"Smoother, Maggie!" Mrs. Harris called across the studio. "And stand up straight!"

Maggie felt heat rush up her face. That was another reason why she and ballet classes did not go together. Mrs. Harris was always pointing out her mistakes.

Maggie did what she was told. She straightened her shoulders. She held her head up high. She flung her arms out beside her.

She spun and spun and spun and spun. Then she crashed right into Ellen.

"Pay attention!" Mrs. Harris said. She clapped her hands twice.

"Sorry," Maggie whispered to Ellen.

Ellen giggled. "It's not a big deal," she whispered back. "At least class is almost over."

"I know!" Maggie said. "I can't wait."

After class, she and Shannon would head to the rink. There, they would skate for about an hour. Mr. Petrov would split his time between the two of them.

Maggie always wished she had her own skating instructor, but she knew that good skating instructors were hard to find. The lessons cost a lot of money, too.

Mr. Petrov was an excellent instructor. Maggie knew she was lucky to be his student.

Finally, ballet class ended. Maggie walked over to her gym bag against the wall. She pulled out a purple sweat jacket and sweat pants and slipped them on. Then she walked from the studio with Ellen and Shannon.

As they walked through the halls of the dance academy, they passed many rooms full of dancers. Music drifted through the doorways.

In front of one room, a song came through the open doorway. Maggie stopped and looked in. The dancers inside were amazing. The music seemed to flow through them and into their bodies.

As she watched the dancers, Maggie suddenly knew. She knew she'd found it.

This was her song.

A Certain Lucas

A Certain Lucas

by

JULIO CORTÁZAR

TRANSLATED FROM THE SPANISH

BY GREGORY RABASSA

Alfred A. Knopf   New York   1984

Library of Congress Cataloging in Publication Data
Cortázar, Julio. A certain Lucas.
Translation of: Un tal Lucas.
I. Title.
PQ7797.C7145T313   1984   863   83–48850
ISBN 0–394–50723–1

Propos de mes Parents:
—Pauvre Léopold!
Maman:
—Coeur trop impressionable . . .
Tout petit, Léopold était déjà singulier.
Ses jeux n'étaient pas naturels.
A la mort du voisin Jacquelin, tombé
d'un prunier, il a fallu prendre des
précautions. Léopold grimpait dans les
branches les plus mignonnes de l'arbre
fatal . . .
A douze années, il circulait imprudement
sur les terrasses et donnait tout son bien.
Il recueillait les insectes morts dans le jardin
et les alignait dans des boîtes de
coquillages ornées de glaces intérieures.
Il écrivait sur des papiers:
Petit scarabée—mort.
Mante religieuse—morte.
Papillon—mort.
Mouche—morte . . .
Il accrochait des banderoles aux arbres du
jardin. Et l'on voyait les papiers blancs

se balancer au moindre souffle du vent
sur les parterres de fleurs.
Papa disait:
—Etudiant inégal . . .
Coeur aventureux, tumultueux et faible.
Incompris de ses principaux camarades et
de Messieurs les Maîtres.
Marqué du destin.

. . . .
Papa et Maman:
—Pauvre Léopold!

MAURICE FOURRÉ
La Nuit du Rose-Hôtel

A Certain Lucas

I

Lucas, His Battles with
the Hydra

Now that he's growing old he realizes that it's not easy to kill it.

It's easy being a hydra but killing it isn't, because if it's really necessary to kill the hydra by cutting off its several heads (between seven and nine according to authors or bestiaries worthy of consultation), at least one has to be left, because the hydra is Lucas himself and what he'd like to do is get out of the hydra but stay in Lucas, to pass from the poly- to the monocephalic. I'd like to see you do it, says Lucas, envying Heracles, who never had such problems with the hydra and who after giving it one clean swipe left it looking like a gaudy fountain with seven or nine jets of blood spouting out of it. It's one thing to kill the hydra and something else again to be that hydra who at one time had been only Lucas and who would like to go back to being him. For example, you take a cut on the head that collects records, and you take another on the one that invariably lays his pipe down on the left-hand side of the desk and the glass with the felt markers on the right and a little to the rear. Now it's time to consider the results.

Hmm, something's been gained, two heads fewer, but the remaining ones in a bit of a crisis as they agitatedly think and think as they face the mournful fact. Or: For a while at least there is a halt in the obsessiveness of that urgent need to complete the series of madrigals by Gesualdo, prince of Venosa (Lucas is missing two records in the series, it seems that they're out of print and won't be reissued, and that lessens the value to him of the other records. Let the head that thinks and wants and gnaws like that die from a clean cut.) Furthermore, it's distressingly novel to reach for the pipe and find that it's not in its place. Let's take advantage of this will for disorder and here and now slice off the head that likes being closed in, having the easy chair for reading beside the lamp, the Scotch at six thirty with two cubes and not much soda, the books and magazines piled up in order of priority.

But it's quite difficult to kill the hydra and get back to Lucas, he can feel it already in the midst of the bloody battle. To begin with, he's describing it on a sheet of paper that he took out of the second drawer on the right-hand side of the desk, when actually there's paper in sight all over the place, but no sir, that's the ritual, and let's not mention the Italian extension lamp four positions a hundred watts placed like a crane over a construction site and most delicately balanced so that the beam of light etc. A flashing slice at that seated Egyptian scribe head. One fewer, oof. Lucas is getting closer to himself, it's starting to look good.

He'll never get to know how many heads he has left to cut off because the phone rings and it's Claudine, who talks about ruuuuunning to the movie theater where they're showing a Woody Allen picture. Evidently Lucas hasn't cut the heads off in the proper ontological order, because his first reaction is no, no way, Claudine is boiling like a crab on the other end, Woody Allen Woody Allen, and Lucas baby, don't push me if you want to win me over, you think I can come down out of this fight that's gushing plasma and Rh factor just because you feel Woody Woody, you've got to understand that there are values and there are values. When from the other end Annapurna is dropped in the form of a receiver onto the cradle, Lucas understands that it would have been better if first he'd killed the head that orders, respects, and hierarchizes time, maybe in that way everything would have softened suddenly and then pipe Claudine markers Gesualdo in different sequences, and Woody Allen, of course. Now it's too late, no Claudine now, not even any words now to go on telling about the battle since there isn't any battle, what head should he cut off since there'll always be another more authoritarian one left, it's time to answer the correspondence that's piling up, in ten minutes the Scotch with its ice and a touch of soda, it's so clear that they've started to grow on him again, that cutting them off was of no use. In the bathroom mirror Lucas can see the complete hydra and its faces with bright smiles, all the teeth show-ing. Seven heads, one for each decade; worse yet, the suspicion that two more may grow on him in con-formity with what certain authorities in hydric matters say, as long as he keeps his health, of course.

Lucas, His Shopping

In view of the fact that Tota has asked him to go down and buy a box of matches, Lucas goes out in his pajamas because the dog days are upon the metropolis, and he settles into fat Muzzio's café where before buying the matches he decides to order an Aperital and soda. He's halfway through that noble aid to digestion when his friend Juárez comes in, also in pajamas, and when he sees him he bursts out that he's got his sister with acute otitis and the druggist won't sell him the tranquilizer drops because there's no prescription and the drops are a kind of hallucinogen that have already zapped more than four hippies in the neighborhood. He knows you and he'll sell them to you, hurry up, Rosita's twisting and turning so much I can't even bear looking at her.

Lucas pays, forgets to buy the matches, and accompanies Juárez to the pharmacy where old Olivetti says no sir, no way, go somewhere else, and at that moment his wife comes out from the back of the store with a camera in her hand and you,

Mr. Lucas, must certainly know how to load it, it's our little girl's birthday and we just now finished the roll, just now finished it. It's just that I've got to bring Tota some matches, Lucas says before Juárez steps on his foot and Lucas offers to load the camera as he understands that old Olivetti will reward him with the ominous drops, Juárez falls apart with gratitude and goes flying out while the wife grabs Lucas and all happy drags him into the birthday party, you're not leaving until you taste the butter cake that Doña Luisa made, many happy returns Lucas says to the little girl who answers with a borborigmy through her fifth slice of cake. They all sing "Happy Birthday" and another toast with orangeade, but the lady brings a little glass of nice cold beer for Mr. Lucas, who is going to take the pictures because they're not very good at it, and Lucas watch the birdy, this one with a flash and this one in the courtyard because the little girl wants the goldfinch in it too, she wants.

"Well," Lucas says, "I'll have to be going because the fact is, Tota . . ."

A phrase left unfinished forever because there is an outburst of shouting in the pharmacy and all kinds of instructions and countermanding. Lucas runs to see and on the way to his escape he runs into the male sector of the Salinsky family and in the middle old man Salinsky, who has fallen out of his chair and whom they're bringing here because they live next door and there's no need to bother the doctor if he hasn't got a fracture of the coccyx or something worse. Stubby Salinsky, who's buddy-buddy with Lucas, grabs him by the pajamas and tells him that the old man is tough but the pavement of the courtyard is tougher, a reason why you can't dismiss a possible fatal fracture since the old man turned green and didn't even think to rub his ass as he usually does. That contradictory detail hasn't escaped old Olivetti who puts his wife on the phone and in less than four minutes there's an ambulance and two attendants, Lucas helps get the old man in because for some reason he'd put his arms around Lucas's neck and ignored his sons completely, and when Lucas is about to get out of the ambulance, the attendants slam the door in his face because they're discussing the soccer game between Boca and Ríver next Sunday and there's no time to be distracted by matters of kinship, so in the end Lucas lands on the floor with the supersonic takeoff and old man Salinsky from his stretcher screw you, young fellow, now you'll see what pain is really like.

At the hospital that's at the other end of the string, Lucas has to explain things, but that's something that takes time in a hospital and are you a member of the family, no, I'm really, but how then, let me explain what happened, fine but let's see your papers, the fact is I'm wearing pajamas, Doctor, your pajamas have got two pockets, agreed but the fact is that Tota, don't tell me this old man's name is Tota, I mean that I had to buy Tota a box of matches and at that point Juárez came in and . . . All right, the doctor sighs, pull down the old man's shorts, Morgada, you can go. I'll stay here until the family gets here and gives me some money for a taxi, Lucas says, I'm not going to get on a bus like this. That all depends, the doctor says, they wear such fantastic clothes today, fashion is versatile, have them X-ray his cubitum, Morgada.

When the Salinskys get out of a taxi, Lucas tells them what's happened and Stubby gives him some dough but at the same time thanks him for five minutes for being such a good neighbor and good friend, suddenly there aren't any taxis anywhere and Lucas, who can't take any more of it, goes off down the street, but it's strange to be walking in pajamas outside of his neighborhood, it had never occurred to him that it's the same as being bare assed, to make things worse not a single stinking bus until the 128 arrives at last and Lucas standing between two girls who look at him in amazement, then from her seat an old lady runs her eyes up and down the stripes of his pajamas as if weighing the decency of that attire which did little to disguise protuberances, Santa Fe and Cánning never comes and rightly so because Lucas has taken a Saavedra bus, then getting off and waiting in a kind of pasture with two small trees and a broken comb, Tota must be like a panther in a washing machine, an hour and a half blessed mother and when the hell is the bus going to come?

It'll probably never come, Lucas tells himself with a kind of sinister enlightenment, this is probably like the withdrawal from Almotásim, thinks Lucas, a cultured man. He almost doesn't see the arrival of the little old toothless lady who comes a little closer to him to ask if by any chance he's got a match.

Lucas, His Patriotism

In the center of the image are probably the geraniums, but there are also wisteria, summer, maté at five thirty, the sewing machine, slippers, and slow conversations about illnesses and family annoyances, a chicken suddenly leaving its calling card between two chairs or the cat after a dove that's way ahead of him. Everything that smells of clothes drying on the line, starch, bluing, and bleach, smells of retirement, of biscuits or fritters, almost always the radio next door with tangos and ads for Geniol, for Cocinero cooking fat the one you should be looking at, and kids kicking a rag ball around the vacant lot out back, Beto made the aerial goal.

Everything so conventional, so pleasant that Lucas out of pure shame looks for other ways out, halfway through the memory he decides to re-member how at that hour he would shut himself up to read Homer and John Dickson Carr, loafing in his little room to avoid hearing again about Aunt Pepa's appendectomy with all the mournful details and the living representation of the horrible nausea brought on by the anesthesia, or the story of the mortgage on the house on the calle Bulnes where Uncle Alejandro was sinking from maté to maté until the apotheosis of collective sighs and everything is going from bad to worse. Josefina, what we need here is a strong government, God damn it. Flora luckily there to show the photo of Clark Gable in the rotogravure of *La Prensa* and remember the starring moments of *Gone with the Wind*. Sometimes Grandmother would remember Francesca Bertini and Uncle Alejandro could see Bárbara La Marr, barbarity unmarred, you and your vamps, you men are all alike, Lucas understands that there's nothing he can do, that he's in the patio again, that the postcard is still stuck forever in the frame of the mirror of time, hand painted, with its fringe of doves, with its thin black border.

Lucas, His Communications

Since he not only writes but likes to go over to the other side and read what others write, Lucas is surprised sometimes at how difficult it turns out to be for him to understand some things. It isn't that they're questions that are particularly abstruse (a horrible word, thinks Lucas, who tends to heft them in the palm of his hand and familiarize himself with them or reject them depending on the color, the smell, or the touch), but suddenly there's something like a dirty pane of glass between him and what he's reading, whence impatience, forced rereading, imminent explosion, and finally the great flight of the magazine or book against the nearest wall with a subsequent fall and a damp plop.

When his reading ends that way, Lucas asks himself what the devil can have happened in the apparently obvious passage from communicator to communicatee. It's hard for him to ask that, because in his case the question is never raised and as rarefied as the air of his reading might be, the more that some things can only come and go after a difficult course, Lucas never ceases to verify whether the coming is valid and whether the going takes place without major obstacles. Little he cares about the individual situation of the readers, because he believes in a mysteriously multiform measurement that in the majority of cases fits like a well-cut suit, and that's why it isn't necessary to give ground in either the coming or the going: between him and the others there will be a bridge as long as what is written is born of a seed and not a graft. In his most delirious inventions there's something that at the same time is so simple, so little bird, and so gin rummy. It's not a matter of writing for others but for oneself, but oneself must also be the others; so elementary, my dear Watson, that it even makes a person mistrust, asking himself if there can't be an unconscious demagogy in that collaboration between sender, message, and receiver. Lucas looks at the word receiver in the palm of his hand, softly strokes its fur, and returns it to its uncertain limbo; he doesn't give a hoot for the receiver since he has him there within range, writing what he reads and reading what he writes, what the great fuck.

Lucas, His Intrapolations

In a documentary and Yugoslavian film one can see how the instinct of the female octopus comes into play to protect her eggs by any means, and among other means of defense she decides to set up her own camouflage by looking for algae, piling them up and hiding behind them so as not to be attacked by morays during the two months that the incubation lasts.

Like everybody, Lucas looks at images anthropomorphically: the octopus *decides* to protect herself, she *looks for* the algae, she *places* them in front of her refuge, she *hides*. But all that (which in a first attempt at an equally anthropomorphic explanation was called *instinct* for lack of something better) happens outside of all consciousness as rudimentary as it might be. If for his part Lucas makes the effort to look on also as from outside, what is left for him? A *mechanism* as alien to the possibilities of his empathy as the moving of the pistons in embolisms or the slipping of a liquid down an inclined plane.

Considerably depressed, Lucas tells himself that at this point the only thing that fits is a kind of intrapolation: this, too, what he's thinking at this moment, is a mechanism that his consciousness thinks it understands and controls; this, too, is an anthropomorphism applied ingenuously to man.

"We're nothing," Lucas thinks for himself and for the octopus.

Lucas, His Disconcertedness

Back there in the dim, dead days Lucas used to go to a lot of concerts and all that Chopin, Zoltán Kodály, Pucciverdi and why am I telling you Brahms and Beethoven and even Ottorino Respighi at moments of weakness.

Now he never goes and fixes things up with records or the radio or whistling memories, Menuhin and Friedrich Gulda and Marian Anderson, things somewhat Paleolithic in these accelerated times, but the truth is that at concerts things were going from bad to worse for him until there was a gentleman's agreement between Lucas who stopped going and the ushers and part of the public who stopped kicking him out. To what was such a spasmodic discord owed? If you ask him, Lucas will remember a few things, for example the night at the Colón when a pianist at the time for encores threw himself with his hands full of Khatchaturian at a completely defenseless keyboard, an occasion taken advantage of by the audience to concede itself a crisis of hysteria the magnitude of which corresponded precisely to the thunder reached by the artist in his final paroxysms, and there we have Lucas searching for something on the floor among the seats and feeling around everywhere.

"Did you lose something, sir?" inquired the lady between whose ankles Lucas's fingers were proliferating.

"The music, madam," Lucas said, barely a second before Senator Poliyatti delivered the first kick on his ass.

There was, likewise, the evening of Lieder in which a lady delicately took advantage of Lotte Lehmann's pianissimos to give off a cough worthy of the horns in a Tibetan temple, a reason for which at some moment the voice of Lucas was heard to say: "If cows could cough, they'd cough like that lady," a diagnosis that brought on the patriotic intervention of Dr. Chucho Beláustegui and the dragging of Lucas with his face on the floor to his final liberation at the curb of the calle Libertad.

It's hard to enjoy concerts when things like that happen, it's better at home.

Lucas, His Criticism

of Reality

Jekyll knows very well who Hyde is, but the knowledge is not reciprocal. Lucas thinks that almost everybody shares Hyde's ignorance, which helps the city of man keep its order. He himself habitually opts for a univocal version, just plain Lucas, but only for reasons of pragmatic hygiene. This plant is this plant. Dorita= Dorita, just that. Except that you shouldn't fool yourself and who knows what this plant is in another context, and let's leave Dorita out of it because.

Early into erotic games Lucas found one of the first refractants, obliterants, or polarizers of the supposed principle of identity. There, all of a sudden, A is not A, or A is non-A. Regions of extreme delight at nine forty will become disagreeable at half past ten, tastes that exalt delirium would incite vomiting if they were proposed across a tablecloth. This (now) isn't this, because I (now) am not I (the other I).

Who changes there, in a bed or in the cosmos: the perfume or the one who smells it? The objective-subjective relationship doesn't interest Lucas; in one case as in another, defined terms escape his definition, Dorita A is not Dorita A, or Lucas B is not Lucas B. And starting from an instantaneous relationship A=B, or B=A, the fission of the crust of the real is given in a chain. Perhaps when the papillae of A rub delectably against the mucosae of B, *everything* is rubbing against something else and playing another game and scorching dictionaries. The time for a moan, of course, but Hyde and Jekyll look at each other face to face in a relationship of A→B / B→A. That jazz song of the forties wasn't far off, "Doctor Hekyll and Mister Jyde." . . .

Lucas, His Spanish Classes

At Berlitz, where they took him on half out of pity, the director, who is from Astorga, warns him against any Argentinisms, not to mention Galliclysms, we teach it proper here, bloody proper, and the first *che* I catch you with means you can hop it. What you will do is teach them to speak in a normal way and none of your fancy frills, because what these Frenchmen are coming here to learn is not to make asses out of themselves at the border or in restaurants. Proper and practical, get that into what we might call your noggin.

Lucas, perplexed, immediately tries to find some texts that would respond to such an illustrious criterion, and when he begins his class in front of a dozen Parisians avid for an *olé* and an I should like an omelette with six eggs, he passes out some photocopies he has made of a passage from an article in *El País*, September 17, 1978, note how modern and how, by his lights, it should be the quintessence of the proper and the practical since

it deals with bullfighting and all the Frenchmen
are thinking about is rushing off to a bullring as
soon as they have their diplomas in their pockets,
one reason why this vocabulary will be exceedingly
useful at the moment of the first of the three stages,
the banderillas, and all the rest. The text reads as
follows, to wit:

The monster, magnificent, medium-sized,
but with spirit, quite well armed with tapering
horns, improved by breeding, for he was noble,
was following the flight of the muleta that the
master from Salamanca manipulated with ease
and control. Relaxed in his posture, he strung
together his passes with the muleta, and each
one was a piece of absolute mastery, making the
bull follow a semicircle about him to the right,
and the conclusion, clean and precise, leaving
the beast at just the right distance. There were
incomparable naturals and tremendous chest
passes, and the help of two-handed ups and
downs, and sign-off passes, but engraved in our
eyes is a natural coupled to a chest pass and the
pattern of the last, ending up at the opposite
shoulder, must figure among the best muleta
work ever done by El Viti.

As is natural, the students immediately fall upon
their dictionaries to translate the passage, a task that

after three minutes is followed by a growing distress, an exchange of dictionaries, a rubbing of eyes and questions for Lucas, which he won't answer at all because he has decided to apply the self-teaching method and in such cases the teacher should gaze out the window while the exercises are being done. When the director appears to inspect Lucas's performance, everyone has left after letting it be known in French what they think of Spanish and especially of dictionaries that have cost them their good francs. The only one remaining is an erudite-looking young man who is asking Lucas if the reference to "the master from Salamanca" could be an allusion to Fray Luis de León, to which Lucas replies that it might well be, although the surest answer is who knows. The director waits for the student to leave and tells Lucas that there's no need to start with classical poetry, of course Fray Luis and all that, but try to find something simpler, let's say something bloody typical like a visit by tourists to a restaurant or a bullring, you'll soon see how they'll get interested and learn overnight.

Lucas, His Ecological
Meditations

In these times of a disheveled and touristy return to Nature, in which city people view country life the way Rousseau viewed the noble savage, I join ranks more than ever with: (a) Max Jacob, who in reply to an invitation to spend a weekend in the country, said, somewhere between stupefaction and terror: "The country? That place where chickens run around raw?"; (b) Dr. Johnson, who halfway through an outing in Greenwich Park energetically expressed his preference for Fleet Street; (c) Baudelaire, who elevated love for the artificial to the notion of Paradise itself.

A landscape, a stroll through the woods, a dousing in a waterfall, a road between two cliffs, can only raise us up to aesthetic heights if we have the assurance of a return home or to the hotel, the lustral shower, dinner and wine, the talk over coffee and dessert, a book or some papers, the eroticism that sums everything up and starts it up again. I don't trust admirers of nature who every so often get out of the car to look at the view and take five or six leaps up onto the rocks; as for the others, those lifetime Boy Scouts who are accustomed to wandering about covered by enormous knapsacks and wild beards, their reactions are mostly monosyllabic or exclamatory; everything seems to consist of standing time and time again looking at a hill or a sunset, which are the most recurrent things imaginable.

Civilized people are lying when they fall into bucolic rapture; if they miss their Scotch on the rocks at seven thirty in the evening, they'll curse the minute they left home to come and endure gnats, sunburn, and thorns; as for those closest to nature, they're as stupid as it is. A book, a play, a sonata, don't need any return or shower; that's where we reach the greatest heights, where we are the most we can be. What the intellectual or the artist who takes refuge in the countryside is looking for is tranquility, fresh lettuce, and oxygenated air; with nature surrounding him on all sides, he reads or paints in the perfect light of a well-oriented room; if he goes out for a walk or goes to the window to look at the animals or the clouds, it's because he's tired with his work or with his ease. Don't trust, then, the absorbed contemplation of a tulip when the contemplator is an intellectual. What's there is tulip + distraction or tulip + meditation (almost never about the tulip). You will never find a natural scene that can take more than five minutes of determined contemplation, and, on the other hand, you will feel all time abolished in the reading of Theocritus or Keats, especially in the passages where scenes of nature appear. Yes, Max Jacob was right: chickens should be cooked.

Lucas, His Soliloquies

Well, it's fine for your brothers to have skinned me until I had it up to here, but now that I've been waiting and wanting so much to go out walking, you arrive soaked to the skin and with that face somewhere between a lead sinker and an umbrella turned inside-out that I've seen on you so many times. There's no way of reaching an understanding like that, you realize. What kind of walk will it be if all I have to do is look at you to tell that I'm going to get drenched along with you, that water will run down my neck, and that the cafés will smell of dampness and there'll almost certainly be a fly in my glass of wine?

It would seem that making a date with you is no good, and the way I prepared it so slowly, first sending your brothers off into a corner since, as always, they do everything possible to bore me, making me lose the wish I've got for you to come and bring me a little fresh air, a moment of sunny corners, and parks with kids and tops. One by one, without consideration, I went along ignoring them

so they wouldn't tilt the scales on me, as is their
wont, abusing the telephone, the urgent letters, that
way they have of appearing at eight o'clock in the
morning and planting themselves for the whole
harvest. I was never rude to them, I even made an
effort to treat them with gentility, simply pretending
that I didn't notice their pressures, the permanent
extortion that they inflict on me from all angles, as
if they were envious about you, wanted to tarnish
you in advance in order to take away my desire to
see you arrive, go out with you. We already know,
the family, but now it happens that instead of
being on my side against them, you too have joined
them without giving me time for anything, not even
to resign myself and contemporize, you appear like
that, dripping water, water that's gray from storm
and cold, a withering negation of what I'd so hoped
for while I was gradually getting on top of your
brothers and trying to keep my strength and happiness, having my pockets full of coins, planning
itineraries, fried potatoes at that restaurant under
the trees where it's so nice to have lunch among the
birds and the girls and old Clemente who recom-
mends the best provolone and sometimes plays the
accordion and sings.

Excuse me if I tell you that you're disgusting,
now I've got to convince myself that it's in the
family, that you're no different although I always
hoped that you'd be the exception, that moment

when everything heavy stops so that lightness can enter, the froth of chatting and turning corners; you see, it's even worse, you appear just the opposite of my hopes, you cynically rap on my window and you wait there for me to put on my rubbers, to take out my raincoat and umbrella. You're the accomplice of the rest of them, I, who knew you were different so many times, loved you for that, you have done the same thing three or four times already, what good is it going to do me for you to answer my desire every so often if this is how it ends up, seeing you there with your hair in your eyes, your fingers dripping gray water, looking at me without speaking. Your brothers are almost better in the end; at least fighting against them helps time pass for me, everything goes better when freedom and hope are being defended; but you, you only give me this emptiness of staying home, of knowing that everything oozes hostility, that night will come like a train that's late on a windswept platform, that it will only come after many matés, many TV news reports, with your brother Monday waiting behind the door for the time when the alarm clock will put me face to face with the one who's the worst, clinging to you but you now again so far from him, behind Tuesday and Wednesday and etc.

Lucas, His New Art of
Giving Lectures

"Ladies, young ladies, etc.
It is a great honor for me, etc. In this hall renowned
for, etc. Please permit me at this moment, etc. I
cannot begin my talk without, etc.

"One should try, above all, to lay out with the
greatest precision possible the meaning and extent
of the theme. There is something bold in all refer-
ences to the future when the mere notion of the
present is presented as uncertain and fluctuating,
when the space-time continuum in which we are
the phenomena of an instant that returns to
nothingness in the very act of conceiving it is more
a working hypothesis than a certainty that can be
corroborated. But without falling into a regressivism
that renders the most elementary operations of the
spirit doubtful, let us make an effort to admit the
reality of a present and even of a history that locates
us collectively with sufficient guarantee as to project
its stable elements and above all its dynamic factors
with sights set on a vision of the future of Honduras
in the collectivity of Latin American democracies.
On the immense continental stage (*hand move-*

ment taking in the whole hall) a small country like Honduras (*hand movement taking in the surface of the table*) represents only one of the multicolored tiles that make up the great mosaic. This fragment (*patting the table with more attention and looking at it with the expression of a person who is seeing something for the first time*) is strangely concrete and evasive at the same time, like all expressions of matter. What is this I am touching? Wood, of course, and in its totality a voluminous object located between you and me, something that in some way separates us with its dry and cursed cut of mahogany. A table! But what's this? One can feel clearly that down here, between these four legs, there is a hostile zone, even more insidious than the solid parts; a parallelopiped of air, like an aquarium of transparent jellyfish that conspire against us, while here above (*he passes his hand over as if to convince himself*) everything is still flat and slippery and absolutely Japanese spy. How shall we understand each other, separated by so many obstacles? If that lady half-asleep who looks extraordinarily like a mole with indigestion would care to get under the table and explain to us the results of her explorations, perhaps we would be able to wipe out the barrier that obliges me to speak to you as if I were sailing from the dock at Southampton on board the *Queen Mary*, a ship that I have always had hopes of traveling on, and with a handkerchief soaked in tears and Yardley lavender to wave the only message still possible to the box seats piled up lugubriously on the pier. A despicable hiatus among all others, why did the board of directors put out this table that's like an obscene sperm whale? It's useless, sir, to offer to take it away, because an unresolved problem returns by way of the unconscious, as has been pointed out so well by Marie Bonaparte in her analysis of the case of Madame Lefèvre, who murdered her daughter-in-law in an automobile. I thank you for your kind gesture and your muscles all ready for action, but I think it essential that we not go into the nature of this indescribable dromedary, and I can see no other solution except facing in hand-to-hand combat, you on your side and I on mine, the ligneous censorship that slowly twists its abominable cenotaph. Out, out, obscurantist object! It's not leaving, that's evident. An axe, an axe! It isn't the least bit frightened, it has the agitated air of immobility of the worst machinations of negativism that surreptitiously inserts itself into the workings of the imagination so as not to let it fly up without a counterweight of mortality to the clouds, which would be its true homeland if gravity, that omnimodous and ubiquitous table, did not weigh so heavily on all your vests, on the buckle of my belt, and even on the lashes of that loveliness who from the fifth row has done nothing but beg me silently to introduce her without wasting time on Honduras. I see signs of impatience, the ushers are furious, there will be resignations on the board of directors, I foresee from now on a reduction in the budget for cultural activities; we are entering entropy, the word is like a swallow falling into a pot of tapioca, nobody knows any longer what's going on and that's precisely what this son-of-a-bitch table wants, to be left alone in an empty hall while we all weep or beat each other up on the exit stairs. Will you triumph, repugnant basilisk? Let no one pretend to ignore this presence that tints all communication, all semantics, with unreality. Look at it, fastened between us, between us on every side of this horrendous wall with the air that reigns in an idiot asylum when a progressive director tries to make Stockhausen's music known. Ah, we thought we were free, somewhere the madam president of the athenaeum was holding ready a bouquet of roses that were to be given me by the secretary's youngest daughter while with fervent applause you reestablished the halted circulation of your behinds. But none of that will happen through the fault of this abominable concretion that we ignored, that we looked upon as we came in as something ever so obvious until a chance brush of my hand suddenly revealed it in its crouching aggressive hostility. How could we imagine a nonexistent freedom, sitting down here when nothing was conceivable, nothing was possible, if first we didn't free ourselves from this table? Slimy molecule of a gigantic enigma, adhesive witness of the worst kind of slavery! Just the idea of Honduras sounds like a balloon bursting at the height of a children's party. Who can now conceive of Honduras, can that word have any meaning while we are on both sides of this river of black fire? And I was going to give a lecture! And you were ready to listen to it! No, it's too much, let us at least have the courage to wake up or at least admit that we want to wake up and that the only thing that can save us is the almost unbearable valor of passing our hand over this indifferent geometric obscenity, while we say all together: It measures 3.2 meters across and 6.40 meters lengthwise, more or less, it's made of solid oak, or mahogany, or varnished pine. But will we ever come to a conclusion, will we know what this is? I don't think so, it will be useless. Here, for example, something that looks like a knot in the wood. Do you think, madam, that it's a knot in the wood? And here, what we call the leg—what is the meaning of this drop at a right angle, this fossilized vomit onto the floor? And the floor, that security for our steps, what does it hide under its polished parquet? . . ."

In general the lecture ends—is ended—much sooner, and the table remains alone in the empty hall. No one, of course, will see it lift up a leg, as tables always do when they are alone.

Lucas, His Hospitals (I)

Since the hospital they have put Lucas into is a five-star hospital, the-patient-is-always-right, and telling them no when they ask for absurd things is a serious problem for the nurses, each one nicer than the next and almost always saying yes for the aforesaid reasons.

Of course it isn't possible to accede to the request of the fat man in room 12, who in the midst of his cirrhosis of the liver demands a bottle of gin every three hours; but on the other hand with what pleasure, what enthusiasm, the girls say yes, of course, indeed, when Lucas, who has gone into the hall while they air out his room and has discovered a bouquet of daisies in the waiting room, asks almost timidly if they would let him take a daisy to his room to cheer up the atmosphere.

After laying the flower down on the night table, Lucas pushes the button and requests a glass of water so as to give the daisy a more fitting posture. As soon as they bring him the glass and fix the flower for him, Lucas points out that the night table is loaded with bottles, magazines, cigarettes, and postcards, so maybe they could place a little table at the foot of the bed, a location that would permit him to enjoy the presence of the daisy without having to dislocate his neck in order to make it out among all the different objects that proliferate on the night table.

The nurse immediately brings what was asked for and puts the glass with the daisy at the most favorable visual angle, something that Lucas thanks her for, pointing out as he does so that since a lot of friends come to visit him and there's a lack of chairs, there would be no better way to take advantage of the presence of the little table than to add two or three comfortable easy chairs and create an atmosphere more conducive to conversation.

As soon as the nurses appear with the chairs, Lucas tells them that he feels exceedingly obliged toward his friends who have spent so much time drinking with him, a reason for which the table would serve perfectly, after first laying a small tablecloth, to hold two or three bottles of whiskey and half a dozen glasses, cut glass if possible, not to mention a Thermos jug with ice and some bottles of soda.

The girls scatter in search of those implements and arrange them artistically on the table, during which occasion Lucas takes the liberty to point out that the presence of glasses and bottles reduces considerably the aesthetic efficacy of the daisy, rather lost in the collection of things, although the solution is quite simple because what's really needed in this room is a closet for clothes and shoes, piled crudely up in a sideboard in the hallway, whereby all that has to be done is to place the glass with the daisy on top of the closet so the flower could dominate the environment and give it that somewhat secret charm that's the key to all good conversation.

Surpassed by the events, but faithful to the norms of the hospital, the girls laboriously drag in a huge closet on which the daisy finally alights like an eye slightly stupefied but full of benevolence. The nurses climb up by the closet and put a little fresh water in the glass, and then Lucas closes his eyes and says now everything is perfect and that he's going to try to sleep for a while. As soon as they close the door he gets up, takes the daisy out of the glass, and throws it out the window, because it's not a flower that he particularly likes.

II

. . . papers where there are sketches of landings in countries not located in either time or space, like the parading of a Chinese military band between eternity and nothingness.

JOSÉ LEZAMA LIMA
Paradiso

The Fate of Explanations

Somewhere there must be a garbage dump where explanations are piled up.

One disquieting thing in this proper panorama: what would happen on the day someone also succeeds in explaining the dump.

The Silent Copilot

The curious union of a story and a hypothesis many years and many miles apart; something that can be a precise fact now, but which until a chance conversation in Paris didn't take shape twenty years *before* on a lonely highway in the province of Córdoba in Argentina.

Aldo Franceschini told the story and I advanced the hypothesis, and both took place in a painter's studio on the rue Paul Valéry amidst glasses of wine, tobacco, and that pleasure of talking about things from out of our homeland without the worthy folkloric sighs of so many other Argentines who hang around without really knowing why. I think it started with the Gálvez brothers and the poplars in Uspallata; in any case, I mentioned Mendoza and Aldo, who comes from there, got all excited, and when we came to he was already on his way by car from Mendoza to Buenos Aires, passing through Córdoba in the middle of the night, and suddenly he was out of gas and his radiator was dry in the middle of the trip. His story can be fitted into the following words:

"It was a very dark night in a place that was completely deserted, and all that could be done was to wait for a car to pass and get us out of our trouble. In those times it was rare not to carry spare gas and water for such long stretches; at worst, the passing car could take my wife and me to a hotel in the first town that had one. We stayed there in the dark, smoking and waiting, the car well off the road. Around one o'clock we saw a car coming on the way to Buenos Aires, and I started to signal with the flashlight in the middle of the road.

"Things like that can't be understood or proved at the moment, but before the car stopped I sensed that the driver didn't want to, that in the car that was coming at full speed there was a kind of wish to keep on going even if what they'd seen was me stretched out on the road with my head cracked open. I had to jump aside at the last moment because the reluctant brakes carried it a hundred feet farther on; I ran to catch up with it and went up to the driver's side. I'd turned the flashlight off because the light from the dashboard was enough to outline the face of the man driving. I quickly explained what the trouble was and asked him for help, and while I was doing it my stomach tightened, because, the fact is, as soon as I approached that car I'd begun to feel fear, an unreasonable fear, because the man in the car should have been the nervous one in that darkness and that place. While I was explaining things to him I looked inside the car, no one was riding in back, but something was sitting on the other front seat. I say 'something' for lack of a better word and because everything started and ended so fast that the only thing that really stood out was a fear like I'd never felt before. I swear to you that when the driver brutally raced the motor while he said 'We haven't got any gas' and started up at the same time, I felt kind of relieved. I went back to my car; I couldn't have explained to my wife what had happened, but I explained it just the same and she understood the absurdity of it, as if what threatened us from that car had reached her too over that distance and without her seeing what I had seen.

"Now you'll probably ask me what I had seen, and I don't know either. Next to the driver something was sitting, I already told you, a black shape that didn't make the slightest movement and didn't turn its head toward me. Actually, nothing should have stopped me from turning on the flashlight to light up the two passengers, but tell me why my arm was incapable of making that movement, why everything only lasted a few seconds, why I almost thanked God when the car started up and disappeared down the highway, and, most of all, why the hell I didn't complain about spending the night in the middle of nowhere until dawn, when a truck driver gave us a hand and even a few drinks of grappa.

"What I'll never understand is everything that went on before I saw anything, which was also practically nothing. It was as if I'd already been afraid when I sensed that the ones in the car didn't want to stop and that they only did when they were forced to, so they wouldn't run me down; but that's not an explanation, because, after all, nobody likes to be stopped in the middle of the night and in a lonely place like that. I've come to convince myself that it all started while I was talking to the driver, and yet it's possible that something had already reached me in some other way while I was going up to the car, a feeling, if you want to call it that. I can't understand any other way why I felt all frozen while I exchanged those words with the man behind the wheel, and how the glimpse of *the other one*, where my fright was immediately concentrated, was the real reason for it all. But to understand anything beyond that . . . Was it a monster, some horrifying cretin he was transporting in the middle of the night so no one would see it? A sick person with a face that was deformed or full of pustules, some abnormal creature irradiating a malignant force, an unbearable emanation? I don't know, I just don't know. But I've never been more afraid in my whole life, old man."

Since I had been carrying about thirty-eight years of neatly stacked Argentine memories, Aldo's story made a click somewhere and the computer shook for a moment and finally produced a card with the hypothesis, maybe the explanation. I even remembered that I'd felt something like that too the first time they'd talked about it, in a café in Buenos Aires, a purely mental fear, like watching *Vampyr* at the movies; many years later that fear could be understood along with Aldo's and, as always, that understanding gave its whole strength to the hypothesis.

"What was riding alongside the driver that night was a dead man," I told him. "It's strange that you'd never heard of the corpse-transporting business in the thirties and forties, especially of tuberculars who'd died in sanatoriums in Córdoba and whose families wanted to bury them in Buenos Aires. Federal taxes or something like that made the transfer of the corpse extremely expensive; so someone got the idea of putting a little makeup on the stiff, seating it beside the driver, and making the run from Córdoba to Buenos Aires in the middle of the night in order to reach the capital before dawn. When they told me about that business I felt the same as you; later on I tried to imagine the lack of imagination on the part of the guys who earned their living that way, and I never could. Can you see yourself in a car with a dead man leaning against you, speeding along at seventy miles an hour through the solitude of the pampas? Five or six hours in which so many things could happen, because a corpse isn't the rigid entity people think it is, and a living person can't be as pachydermic as people are also led to believe."

A more pleasant corollary while we have another little drink of wine: at least two of the people who were in that business subsequently went on to be famous drivers in road racing. And it's funny, now that I think about it, that this conversation had started with the Gálvez brothers; I don't think they were in that business, but they raced against others who had been. It's also true that in those mad races they always traveled with a dead man clinging close to their bodies too.

It Could Happen to Us,
Believe Me

The *verba volant* seems more or less acceptable to them, but what they can't tolerate is the *scripta manent,* and thousands of years have already passed this way, so just imagine. That's why that big shot was enthusiastic over the news that a rather unknown savant had invented the string stretcher and was selling it almost for nothing because in the last days of his life he'd become a misanthrope. He received him the very same day and offered him tea and toast, which is the proper thing to offer savants.

"I'll come right to the point," the guest said. "For you, literature, poems, and things like that, right?"

"That's it, Doctor," said the big shot. "And pamphlets, opposition newspapers, all that shit."

"Perfect, but you must realize that the invention doesn't make distinctions; I mean, your own press, your hacks . . ."

"We can't help that, but in any case I'll come out ahead if it's true."

"In that case," the savant said, taking a small apparatus out of his vest, "it's a simple matter.

What's a word but a series of letters and what's a letter but a line that takes on a given shape? Now that we're agreed, I push this little mother-of-pearl button and the apparatus turns loose the stretcher that works on each letter and leaves it flattened out and smooth, a horizontal string of ink. Shall I do it?"

"Do it, God damn it," roared the big shot.

The daily government report on the table ostentatiously changed its appearance: page after page of columns filled with little dashes like some idiot Morse code that said only − − − − − − − − − −.

"Take a peek at the *Encyclopaedia Britannica*," said the savant, who was not unaware of the sempiternal presence of that artifact in governmental environments. But it wasn't necessary because the telephone was already ringing, the minister of culture came bouncing in, the square was full of people, that night all over the planet not a single printed book, not a single letter was left at the bottom of a printer's box.

And I can write this because I am the savant and also because there's no rule that doesn't have its exception.

Family Ties

They hate Aunt Angustias so much that they even take advantage of vacations to let her know it. No sooner has the family gone off in different tourist directions than there's a flood of postcards in Agfacolor, Kodachrome, even in black and white if the others aren't available, but all, without exception, loaded with insults. From Rosario, from San Andrés de Giles, from Chivilcoy, from the far reaches of Chacabuco and Moreno, the postmen five or six times a day cursing, Aunt Angustias happy. She never leaves her house, she likes to stay in the courtyard, she spends her day getting postcards and is enchanted.

Some sample postcards: "Greetings, loathsome, drop dead—Gustavo." "I spit in your knitting, Josefina." "I hope the cat piss dries up your geraniums, your little sister." And so on.

Aunt Angustias gets up early to take care of the postmen and tip them. She reads the cards, admires the photographs, and reads the greetings again. At night she takes out her souvenir album and goes about placing the day's harvest very carefully in it so that not only the scenes are visible but also the greetings. "Poor angels, all the postcards they send me!" Aunt Angustias thinks. "This one with the little cow, this one with the church, here Lake Traful, here the bouquet of flowers," looking at them one by one with tender emotion and sticking pins into each card so they won't ever fall out of the album, although, this too, always sticking them through the signature, who can say why.

How Come One Goes By?

Important discoveries are made under the most unusual circumstances and in the most unusual places. Newton's apple—how's that for something to be flabbergasted at? It happened that way with me when in the middle of a business meeting, without knowing why, I thought about cats—who had nothing to do with the order of business—and I suddenly discovered that cats are telephones. Just like that, as always in matters of genius.

A discovery like that, of course, arouses certain surprise, since no one is accustomed to having telephones coming and going and above all having them drink milk and like fish. It takes time to understand that it's a matter of special telephones, like walkie-talkies, which don't have any wires, and also that we're special too in the sense that up until now we haven't understood that cats are telephones and therefore it hasn't occurred to us to use them.

Given the fact that this negligence goes back to remotest antiquity, little can be expected of the communication system we might succeed in establishing after my discovery, because it's rather evident that there's no code that would permit us to understand the messages, their origin, and the nature of the people sending them to us. It's not a question, as has probably been noticed, of picking up a nonexistent tube to dial a number that has nothing to do with our figures, and much less understand what they might be trying to tell us from the other end with some equally confusing motive. That the telephone works is proven by every cat with an honesty that is poorly rewarded by biped subscribers; no one can deny that his black or white, brindle or Angora telephone always enters with a decisive air, stops at the feet of the subscriber, and produces a message that our primitive and pathetic literature transliterates stupidly in the form of *meow* and other similar phonemes. Silk verbs, felt adjectives, sentences simple and compound but always as smooth as soap and glycerine form a discourse that is sometimes related to hunger, in which case the telephone is nothing but a cat, but at other times it is expressed with an absolute lack of personal need, which proves that a cat is a telephone.

Clumsy and pretentious, we have let millennia go by without answering the calls, without wondering where they were coming from, who was on the other end of that line which a twitching tail grew tired of showing us in houses all over the world.

What good does my discovery do me or any of us? Every cat is a telephone, but every man is just a poor man. Who can say what they keep on telling us, the paths they're showing us; for my part I've only been capable of dialing on my ordinary telephone the number of the university where I work and announcing my discovery almost with shame. It seems useless to mention the silence of congealed tapioca with which it was received by the scholars who answer that kind of call.

A Small Paradise

The forms of happiness are quite varied, and one shouldn't be surprised that the inhabitants of the country governed by General Orangu have considered themselves happy, starting with the day they had their blood filled with little gold fishes.

Actually, the little fishes aren't gold but merely gilded, but it takes only one look for their resplendent leaps to be immediately translated into an anxious urge for possession. The government was quite aware of it when a naturalist captured the first specimens, who reproduced quickly in a propitious culture broth. Technically known as Z-8, the little gold fish is exceedingly small, to such a degree that if it were possible to imagine a hen the size of a fly, the little fish would be the size of that hen. Therefore it is quite simple to incorporate it into the blood torrent of the inhabitants of the country at the time they reach the age of eighteen; that age and the corresponding technical procedure are fixed by law.

That's why all young people in the country wait anxiously for the day when it will be their turn to go into an implantation center and their families surround them with the joy that always accompanies great ceremonies. A vein in the arm is connected to a tube that comes down from a transparent flask filled with physiological serum in which, when the moment arrives, twenty little gold fishes are placed. The family and the one being benefited can admire at their leisure the leaps and twists of the little gold fishes in the glass flask until, one after the other, they're swallowed by the tube, descending motionless and a little bewildered perhaps like so many more drops of light, to disappear into the vein. A half-hour later the citizen is in possession of his complete number of little gold fishes and goes off for an extended celebration of his accession to happiness.

Carefully considered, the inhabitants are happy because of imagination rather than direct contact with reality. Although they can no longer see them, they all know that the little gold fishes are coursing through the great tree of their veins and arteries, and before going to sleep, in the concavity of their eyelids, they seem to see the coming and going of the bright sparks, more golden than ever against the red background of the rivers and streams through which they slip along. What fascinates them most is the notion that the twenty little gold fishes won't be long in multiplying, and that's how they picture them, numberless and radiant everywhere, slipping along beneath the forehead, reaching the tips of fingers and toes, concentrating in the large femoral arteries, the jugular vein, or scurrying along in their agile way through the narrowest and most secret zones. The periodic passage through the heart makes for the most delightful image of that inner vision, for there the little gold fishes will find toboggan slides, ponds, and waterfalls for their games and gatherings, and it is certainly in that great noisy port that they recognize each other, choose, and mate. When boys and girls fall in love they do so in the conviction that within their heart some little gold fish has also found its mate. Even certain inciting tickles are attributed to the coupling of the little gold fishes in the zones involved. The essential rhythms of life are therefore, in correspondence inside and out; it would be hard to imagine a more harmonious happiness.

The only obstacle to this picture is the periodic death of one of the little gold fishes. Long-lived as they are, the day must come, nevertheless, when one of them will perish and its body, dragged along by the flow of blood, ends up blocking the passage from an artery to a vein or from a vein to a vessel. The inhabitants of the country know the symptoms, most simple in other respects: breathing becomes difficult and sometimes they feel dizzy. In that case they proceed to make use of one of the injectable ampules that everyone keeps stored at home. In a few minutes the product disintegrates the body of the dead little fish and circulation returns to normal. In line with the foresight of the government, every inhabitant is called upon to use two or three ampules a month, for the little gold fishes reproduce enormously and their death rate tends to rise with time.

General Orangu's government has set the price of each ampule at the equivalent of twenty dollars, which presupposes an annual income of several million; if that seems to be a heavy tax to foreign observers, the inhabitants have never seen it that way, because every ampule returns them happiness and it's only proper for them to pay for it. When it's a matter of families without resources, a very common thing, the government supplies the ampules on credit, collecting for them, as is logical, at twice their retail price. If there are still some who don't have ampules, there is always the recourse to a flourishing black market that the government, understanding and kindhearted, allows to prosper for the greater good of its people and a few colonels. What does misery matter, after all, when it is well known that everyone has his little gold fishes, and that the day will come soon when a new generation will receive theirs in turn and there will be festivals and there will be singing and there will be dancing?

Artistos' Life

When children begin to enter the Spanish language, the general principle of endings in "o" and "a" seems so logical to them that they apply it, without hesitation and with a great deal of logic, to exceptions, and therefore, while Beba is an *idiota*, Toto is an *idioto*, an *águila* and a *gaviota* (an eagle and a gull) set up housekeeping with an *águilo* and a *gavioto*, and there is almost no *galeoto* (galley slave) who has not been put in chains through the fault of a *galeota*. This seems so proper to me that I continue to be convinced that activities such as those of *turista* (tourist), *artista* (artist), *contratista* (contractor), and *escapista* (escapist) ought to take their endings according to the sex of the ones doing them. In a resolutely androcratic civilization like that of Latin America, it is proper to speak of *artistos* in general and *artistos* and *artistas* in particular. As for the lives that follow, they are modest but exemplary, and I shall become enraged with anyone who finds to the contrary.

KITTEN ON THE KEYS

A cat had been taught to play the piano, and this animal, sitting on a stool, played and played the whole existing piano repertory, and in addition five compositions of its own dedicated to several dogs.

Otherwise, the cat was possessed of a perfect stupidity, and during concert intermissions he would compose new pieces with a drive that left everyone flabbergasted. In that way he reached Opus 89, during which he was the victim of a brick thrown by someone with a tenacious rage. He sleeps his final sleep in the lobby of the Great Rex Theater, 640 Corrientes.

NATURAL HARMONY, OR
YOU CAN'T KEEP ON VIOLATING IT

A child had thirteen fingers on each hand, and his aunts immediately put him to playing the harp, something that made good use of the extras, and he completed the course in half the time needed by poor pentadigitates.

After that the child came to play in such a way that there was no score worthy of him. When he began to give concerts, the amount of music that he concentrated in that time and space with his twenty-six fingers was so extraordinary that the audience couldn't keep up and was always behind, so that when the young *artisto* was coming to the end of *The Fountain of Arethusa* (a transcription) the poor people were still in the *Tambourin chinois* (an arrangement). This naturally created horrible confusions, but everyone recognized that the child played like an angel.

So it came to pass that the faithful listeners, the same as box-seat subscribers and newspaper critics, continued going to the child's concerts, earnestly trying not to be left behind as the program went on. They listened so hard that several of them began to grow ears on their faces, and with every new ear that grew on them they got a little closer to the music of the twenty-six fingers on the harp. The trouble came when the Wagnerian concert let out and people on the street fainted by the dozen as they saw listeners appear with their whole visages covered by ears, and then the municipal superintendent took drastic steps and put the child in the typing pool at Internal Revenue, where he worked so fast that it was pleasure for his bosses and death for his co-workers. As for music, in a dark corner of the parlor, forgotten by its owner perhaps, silent and covered with dust, the harp could be seen.

CUSTOMS OF THE SYMPHONY
ORCHESTRA CALLED "THE FLY"

The musical director of the "Fly" Symphony, Maestro Tabaré Piscitelli, was the author of the orchestra's motto: "Creation within freedom." To that end he authorized the use of open collars, anarchism, Benzedrine, and personally set a high example of independence. Hadn't he been observed in the middle of a Mahler symphony to turn the baton over to one of the violinists (who got the fright of his life) and go off to read the newspaper in an empty seat?

The cellists of the "Fly" Symphony loved the harpist, the widow Pérez Sangiácomo, en bloc. This love was translated into a noteworthy tendency to break the order of the orchestra and surround the bewildered performer with a sort of screen of cellists, as her hands stood out like signals for help throughout the whole program. Furthermore, not once did a subscriber to the concerts hear a single arpeggio from the harp, because the steady buzz of the cellos covered up its delicate effusions.

Threatened by the board of directors, Mrs. Pérez Sangiácomo showed a preference in her heart for the cellist Remo Persutti, who was authorized to keep his instrument beside the harp, while the others returned, a sad procession of scarabs, to the place tradition assigns their pensive carapaces.

In this orchestra one of the bassoonists couldn't play his instrument without the strange phenomenon of his being sucked in and immediately expelled out the other end, with such rapidity that the stupefied musician found himself suddenly on the other end of the bassoon and had to turn around with great speed and go on playing, not without the conductor's castigating him with horrendous personal slurs.

One night, when they were playing the *Doll Symphony* by Albert Williams, the bassoonist, in an attack of absorption, found himself suddenly at the other end of the instrument, with the serious inconvenience this time that said point in space was occupied by the clarinetist Perkins Virasoro, who, as a result of the collision, was flung on top of the double basses and arose markedly furious and pronouncing words that no one has ever heard from the mouth of a doll; such at least was the opinion of the lady subscribers and of the fireman on duty in the hall, the father of several little ones.

The cellist Remo Persutti being absent, the personnel of that string section moved as a group over beside the harpist, the widow Pérez Sangiácomo, whence they didn't move for the whole evening. The theatre staff laid down a rug and put potted ferns on it to fill the obvious gap that this produced.

The kettledrummer, Alcides Radaelli, took advantage of the tone poems of Richard Strauss to send messages in Morse code to his sweetheart seated in the loge, left eight.

An army telegrapher present at the concert because of the cancellation of the boxing matches in Luna Park due to a death in the family of one of the fighters, deciphered with great wonderment the following phrase that poured forth halfway through *Also Sprach Zarathustra*: "Are your hives better, Cuca?"

QUINTESSENCES

The tenor Américo Scravellini, of the cast at the Marconi Theater, sang so sweetly that his fans called him "the angel."

So no one was too startled when in the middle of a concert they saw four handsome seraphim descend through the air and with an ineffable whisper of gold and scarlet accompany the voice of the great singer. If one part of the audience showed understandable signs of surprise, the rest, enthralled by the vocal perfection of tenor Scravellini, accepted the presence of the angels as an almost necessary miracle, or, rather, as if it weren't a miracle at all. The singer himself, given over to his effusion, limited himself to lifting his eyes toward the angels, and he kept on singing with that indefinable mezza voce that had made him famous in the whole chain of theaters.

Softly, the angels surrounded him, and holding him with infinite tenderness and ever so gently, they rose up above the stage while the audience trembled with emotion and wonder, and the singer continued on with his melody which became all the more ethereal in the air.

In that way the angels took him away from his public, who finally understood that the tenor Scravellini was not of this world. The celestial group reached the highest point of the theater; the singer's voice was becoming more and more otherworldly. When the final and absolutely perfect note of the aria came out of his throat, the angels dropped him.

Texturologies

Only a brief synthesis is given of the six critical works quoted here and their respective foci.

G*oose Grease*, poems by José Lobizón (La Paz, Bolivia: Horizontes, 1974). Critical review by Michel Pardal in the *Bulletin sémantique*, University of Marseilles, 1975 (translated from the French):

> Few times have we had the opportunity to read such a poverty-stricken product of Latin American poetry. Confusing tradition with creation, the author has put together a sorry litany of commonplaces that the versification only manages to make emptier still.

Article by Nancy Douglas in *The Phenomenological Review*, The University of Nebraska, 1975 (translated from the English):

It is obvious that Michel Pardal is wrong in his handling of the concepts of creation and tradition in the degree that the latter is the decanted sum of a past creation and cannot be placed in opposition in any way to contemporaneous creation.

Article by Boris Romanski in *Sovietskaya Bieli,* Mongolian Writers' Union, 1975 (translated from the Russian):

With a frivolity that does not disguise her real ideological intention, Nancy Douglas piles high her most conservative and reactionary plate of criticism, attempting to slow the advance of contemporary literature in the name of a supposed "fecundity of the past." What has been reproached so long now in Soviet literature becomes dogma in the capitalist camp. Is it not proper, therefore, to speak of frivolity?

Article by Philip Murray in *The Nonsense Tabloid,* London, 1976 (translated from the English):

The language used by Professor Boris Romanski deserves the rather kind description of low-grade jargon. How is it possible to confront the critical intent in perceptibly historicist terms? Does Professor Romanski still ride in a horse-drawn carriage, seal his letters with wax, and cure his colds with leeches? Within the current perspective of criticism, is it not time to replace notions of tradition and creation with symbiotic galaxies such as "historico-cultural entropy" and "anthropodynamic co-efficient?"

Article by Gérard Depardiable in *Quel Sel*, Paris, 1976 (translated from the French):

Albion, Albion, ever true to yourself! It seems incredible that from the other side of a channel across which one can swim there should appear and persist such involutioning toward the most irreversible uchrony of critical space. It is obvious: Philip Murray has not read Saussure, and his apparently polysemous proposals are most definitely just as obsolete as the ones he is criticizing. For us the dichotomy inherent in the continuous apparential of the scripturant movement is projected as the signified in the end and as signifier in virtual implosion (demotically, past and present).

Article by Benito Almazán in *One Track*, Mexico City, 1977 (translated from the Spanish):

An admirable heuristic study, that of Gérard Depardiable, which might well be categorized as structurological because of its double ur-semiotic richness and its conjunctive rigor in a field so propitious for mere epiphonemes. I will let a poet premonitorially sum up these textological conquests that already foretell the parametainfracriticism of the future. In his masterly book *Goose Grease*, José Lobizón states at the end of a long poem:

It is one thing to be a goose because of quills, quite another to be quills of the goose.

How can one add anything to that dazzling absolutization of the contingent?

What Is Polygraphy?

My namesake Casares will never cease to startle me. Given what follows, I was inclined to call this chapter "Polygraphy," but a doglike instinct led me to page 840 of the ideological pterodactyl, and there, boom: On one side a polygraph is, in the second acceptance, "a writer who deals with diverse material," but on the other polygraphy is exclusively the art of writing in such a way that the writing can only be deciphered by someone with a previous knowledge of the key and, also, the art of deciphering writings of that nature. Because of this my chapter cannot be called "Polygraphy," for it deals with nothing less than Dr. Samuel Johnson.

In 1756, at the age of forty-seven and according to data from the dedicated Boswell, Dr. Johnson began his collaboration on *The Literary Magazine, or Universal Review.* Over the period of fifteen monthly numbers the following essays were published: "An Introduction to the Political State of Great Britain," "Remarks on the Militia Bill,"

"Observations on His Britannick Majesty's Treaties with the Empress of Russia and the Landgrave of Hesse Cassel," "Observations on the Present State of Affairs," and "Memoirs of Frederick III, King of Prussia." In that same year and during the first three months of 1757, Johnson reviewed the following books:

Birch's *History of the Royal Society*
Murphy's *Gray's-Inn Journal*
Warton's *Essay on the Writings and Genius of Pope*
Hampton's *Translation of Polybius*
Blackwell's *Memoirs of the Court of Augustus*
Russell's *Natural History of Aleppo*
Sir Isaac Newton's *Arguments in Proof of a Deity*
Borlase's *History of the Isles of Scilly*
Holme's *Experiments on Bleaching*
Browne's *Christian Morals*
Hales's *On Distilling Sea Water, Ventilators in Ships, and Curing an Ill Taste in Milk*
Lucas's *Essays on Waters*
Keith's *Catalogue of Scottish Bishops*
Browne's *History of Jamaica*
Philosophical Transactions, Vol. XLIX
Mrs. Lennox's *Translation of Sully's Memoirs*
Elizabeth Harrison's *Miscellanies*

Evans's *Map and Account of the Middle
Colonies in America*
Letter on the Case of Admiral Byng
Appeal to the People Concerning Admiral Byng
Hanway's *Eight Days' Journey and Essay
on Tea*
The Cadet, A Military Treatise
*Some Further Particulars in Relation to the Case
of Admiral Byng,* by a Gentleman of Oxford
*The Conduct of the Ministry Relating to the
Present War, Impartially Examined*
*A Free Inquiry into the Nature and Origin
of Evil*

In little more than a year, five essays and twenty-
five reviews by a man whose principal defect, according to himself and his critics, was indolence. . . .
Johnson's renowned *Dictionary* was finished in three
years, and there is evidence that the author worked
practically alone on that gigantic task. The actor
Garrick, in a poem, celebrates the fact that Johnson
"has conquered forty Frenchmen," an allusion to
the compilers of the French Academy who worked
in conjunction on the dictionary of their tongue.

I have a great liking for polygraphs who cast their
fishing poles in all directions, pretending at the
same time to be half-asleep like Dr. Johnson, and
who find a way to fulfill a task spread out over such
themes as tea, the correction of bad taste in milk,

and the court of Augustus, not to mention Scottish bishops. When all is said and done, that's what I'm doing with this book, but Dr. Johnson's indolence looks to me like such an inconceivable fury of work that my best efforts won't reach beyond a vague rousing up out of a siesta in a Paraguayan hammock. When I think that there are Argentine novelists who produce a novel every ten years and in the interval convince journalists and distinguished ladies that they are exhausted by their inner work . . .

Railway Observations

Mrs. Cinamomo's awakening is not a happy one, because when she puts her feet into her slippers she discovers they've become full of snails. Armed with a hammer, Mrs. Cinamomo proceeds to squash the snails, after which she finds herself forced to throw the slippers into the garbage. With that intention in mind, she goes down to the kitchen and starts to chat with the maid.

"The house will be so empty now that Ñata's gone."

"Yes, ma'am," says the maid.

"What a crowd of people at the station last night! All the platforms were filled with people. Ñata was so worked up."

"A lot of trains leave," says the maid.

"That's right, child. The railroad goes everywhere."

"That's progress," says the maid.

"The timetables are so exact. The train was to leave at 8:01 and that's just what it did, all filled up."

"That's how it should be," says the maid.

"What a nice compartment Ñata had! You should have seen it—gilded bars all over."

"It must have been first-class," says the maid.

"One part was just like a balcony and it was made of transparent plastic."

"Just imagine," says the maid.

"There were only three people traveling, all with reserved seats, divine little tickets. Ñata had the window seat, beside the gilded bars."

"You don't say," says the maid.

"She was so pleased, she could lean over the balcony and water the plants."

"Were there plants?" says the maid.

"The ones that grow between the tracks. You ask for a glass of water and you water them. Ñata asked for one immediately."

"Did they bring it?" says the maid.

"No," says Mrs. Cinamomo sadly, throwing the slippers full of dead snails into the garbage.

Swimming in a Pool of
Gray Grits

Professor José Migueletes in 1964 invented the pool of gray grits[1] and lent support to the noteworthy technical perfection that he had brought to the art of natation. Nevertheless, the results in the world of sports were not long in coming to notice when, at the Ecological Games in Baghdad, the Japanese champion, Akiro Teshuma, broke the world record by swimming five meters in one minute and four seconds.

---

[1] Which, in case one doesn't know, is finely ground chick-pea flour and which, mixed with sugar, was the delight of Argentine children of my time. There are those who maintain that grits are made from corn, but only the Spanish Academy dictionary says so, and we know all about that. These grits are a grayish powder that comes in little paper bags, which children raise to their mouths with results that tend to end in suffocation. When I was in the fourth grade in Banfield (Southern Rail Line) we would eat so much gray grits during recess that out of thirty pupils only twenty-two of us finished the year. The terrified teachers advised us to take a deep breath before ingesting the grits, but children, I swear, such stubbornness. Having finished explaining the merits and demerits of such a nutritious substance, I ask the reader to climb back up to the top of the page to find out that nobody

Interviewed by enthusiastic journalists, Teshuma affirmed that swimming in grits was far superior to swimming in the traditional H_2O. To begin with, the force of gravity can't be felt, and instead there's more of an effort to sink the body into that soft farinaceous cushion; in that way the initial dive consists mainly of sliding over the grits, and those who know how have a head start of several centimeters over their opponents. From that phase on, the natatorial movements are based on the traditional technique of the spoon in the porridge bowl, while the feet apply a rotation of a cyclistic nature, or, rather, in the manner of venerable paddle-wheeler organs that still ride along in certain movie houses. The problem that demands a quick solution is, as anyone might suspect, that of breathing. Since it has been proven that the backstroke is of no help in advancing over the grits, one has to swim face down, or slightly to one side, because of which the eyes, the nose, the ears, and the mouth are immediately buried in an ever-so-volatile coating which only a few wealthy clubs perfume with powdered sugar. The solution to that passing inconvenience doesn't call for any great complications: contact lenses properly impregnated with silicates can hold off the adherent tendencies of the grits; two wads of gum fix things up on the ear side; the nose is provided with a system of safety valves; and as for the mouth, it can go on its own, since the calculations of the Tokyo Research Center estimate that in a ten-meter race only a few hundred grams of grits are swallowed, which increases the discharge of adrenaline, producing metabolic vivacity and muscular tone, more essential than ever in races like these.

Asked about the reasons why many international athletes show an ever-growing proclivity for swimming in grits, Tashuma would only answer that after several millennia it has finally been proven that there is a certain monotony in the act of jumping into the water and coming out all wet without anything having changed very much in the sport. He let it be understood that the imagination is slowly coming into power and that it's time now to apply revolutionary forms to old sports whose only incentive is to lower records by fractions of a second, when that can be done, which is quite rare. He modestly declared himself unable to suggest equivalent discoveries for soccer and tennis, but he did make an oblique reference to a new development in sports, mentioning a glass ball that may have been used in a basketball game in Naga, and whose accidental but always possible breakage brought on the act of hara-kiri by the whole team whose fault it was. Everything can be expected of Nipponese culture, especially if it sets out to imitate the Mexican. But to limit ourselves to the West and to grits, this last item has begun to demand higher prices, to the particular delight of countries that produce it, all of them in the Third World. The death by asphyxiation of seven Australian children who tried to practice fancy dives in the new pool in Canberra demonstrates, however, the limitations of this interesting product, the use of which should not be carried too far when amateurs are involved.

Now Shut Up,
You Distasteful Adbekunkus

Maybe shellfish aren't neurotic, but from there on up you only have to take a good look; for my part I've seen neurotic hens, neurotic worms, incalculably neurotic dogs; there are trees and flowers that the psychiatry of the future will deal with psychoanalytically because even today their shapes and colors are frankly morbid to us. No one will be puzzled, then, at my indifference when, at the moment of taking a shower, I heard myself mentally, say, in English, with visible vindictive pleasure: *Now shut up, you distasteful Adbekunkus.*

While I was soaping myself, the admonition was repeated rhythmically and without the slightest conscious analysis on my part, almost as if forming part of the lather of my shower. Only at the end, between the cologne and the underwear, did I take an interest in myself and from there in Adbekunkus, whom I had ordered to be quiet with such insistence over the past half an hour. I spent a good night of insomnia asking myself about that slight neurotic manifestation, that inoffensive but insistent out-

burst that went on like a resistance to sleep; I began
to ask myself where this Adbekunkus could be talking and talking until something in me that was
listening would demand peremptorily and in English that he shut up.

I put the fantastic hypothesis aside, too easy:
there was nothing or nobody called Adbekunkus,
endowed with an elocutive and annoying facility.
That it was a question of a proper noun, I didn't
doubt for a moment; there are times when one can
even see the capital letter of certain combinations
of sounds. I know myself to be rather well endowed
as to the invention of words that seem devoid of
meaning or are until I give it to them in my own
way, but I don't think I've ever brought out a name
as unpleasant, as grotesque, as worthy of rejection,
as Adbekunkus. The name of a lesser devil, of a sad
goblin, one of those invoked by many a black book;
a name as distasteful as its owner: *distasteful Adbekunkus.* But employing mere sentiment didn't lead
anywhere; nor, it's true, did analogical analysis,
mnemonic echoes, all associative recourses. I ended
up accepting the fact that Adbekunkus was not
attached to any conscious element; the neurotic part
seemed to be precisely in the fact that the phrase
demanded silence of something, of somebody, who
was a perfect void. How many times does a name
that rises up out of some distraction or other end
up bringing forth an animal or human image? Not

this time. It was necessary for Adbekunkus to be quiet, but he would never be quiet because he had never spoken or shouted. How could I fight against that concretion of void? I fell asleep a little like him, hollow and absent.

Love 77

And after doing every-thing they do, they get up, they bathe, they powder themselves, they perfume themselves, they comb their hair, they get dressed, and so, progres-sively, they go about going back to being what they aren't.

New Items in Public Services

IN A SWIFTIAN MOOD

Persons worthy of belief have let it be known that the author of this report is familiar almost to a neurotic degree with the underground transportation system of the city of Paris and that his tendency to harp on the theme reveals underlying things that are disquieting to say the least. Nevertheless, how can one be quiet about the restaurant that circulates in the Paris subway and arouses contradictory comments in the most diverse circles? No gaudy advertising has brought it to the attention of possible customers; the authorities maintain a silence that is downright uncomfortable and only the slow flow of vox populi oil has smoothed the way so many feet down. It's impossible for an innovation like that to be limited to the privileged perimeters of an urban area that thinks all is permitted it; it's only proper and even necessary for Mexico, Sweden, Uganda, and Argentina, inter alia, to learn about an experience that goes far beyond gastronomy.

The idea must have come from Maxim's, since that temple of grub was awarded the dining-car concession, inaugurated in almost complete silence around the middle of the current year. The decor and the equipment seem to have unimaginatively repeated the atmosphere of any railroad restaurant, except that here one eats infinitely better, although for a price also infinitely, details that will be sufficient for an automatic selection of customers. There are many who wonder in perplexity about the reasons for setting up a business that is refined to such a degree within the context of a means of transportation that is rather working class, as is the subway; others, this writer among them, maintain the disapproving silence that such a question merits, for the answer itself is obviously contained therein. In these high moments of Western civilization there is no longer any great interest in the passage from a Rolls-Royce to a deluxe restaurant, in the midst of gold braid and bows, but it's easy to imagine the quivering delight represented in going down filthy subway stairs to put one's ticket into the slot that permits access to platforms invaded by the quantity, sweat, and crowding of the hordes that leave factories and offices on their way home, and waiting in the midst of berets, caps, and mufflers of doubtful quality for the arrival of the train in which a car appears that common passengers can only contemplate for the brief moment in which it stops. The delight, furthermore, goes far beyond this first and unusual experience, as will be explained shortly.

The motivating idea behind such a brilliant initiative has its antecedents all down through history, from Messalina's expeditions to the Suburra, to the hypocritical strolls by Harun arRashid through the alleyways of Baghdad, not to mention the innate pleasure of all authentic aristocrats in clandestine contact with the worst elements and the American song "Let's Go Slumming." Obliged by their status to travel about in private cars, planes, and first-class railroad coaches, the Parisian *haute bourgeoisie* has finally discovered something that until now had mostly meant certain stairs that lose themselves in the depths and that are taken only on rare occasions and with a marked repugnance. At a time when French workers tend to give up the demands that have made them so famous in our century in order to close their fingers over the steering wheel of a car of their own and to stay glued to the screen of a television set during the little free time they have, who can be scandalized by the fact that the moneyed bourgeoisie turn their backs on things that are threatening to become common and search, with an irony that their intellectuals cannot fail to notice, for a terrain that in appearance brings them as close as possible to the proletariat, and which, at the same time, keeps it much farther away than on the ordinary urban surface? It is no use saying that the restaurant concessionnaires and their clientele itself would be the first to reject indignantly a proposition that would seem ironic in any way; after all, the only thing that's needed to step aboard the restaurant and be served like any other customer is enough money, and it's a well-known fact that many of the beggars who sleep on benches in the subway have huge fortunes—like gypsies and leaders of the Left.

The restaurant management of course shares these rectifications, but that's not why they've ceased taking the measures tacitly demanded by their refined clientele, because money isn't the only entrée to a place founded on decency, good manners, and the indispensable use of deodorants. We might even go so far as to say that this necessary selection made up the basic problem for those in charge of the restaurant, and it wasn't easy to find a solution that was both natural and strict at the same time, for it's common knowledge that subway platforms are open to all, and that there's not that much difference between first- and second-class cars, to the degree that conductors are accustomed to be lax during rush hours and let the first-class cars fill up without checking to see if the passengers have the right to fill them or not. Consequently, channeling the restaurant customers in a way that allows them easy access presents difficulties that seem to have been overcome so far, although those in charge almost never hide the uneasiness that comes over them the minute the train stops at each station. The method, in a general way, consists of keeping the doors closed while the people get in and out of the regular cars, and opening them only for a few seconds before the train leaves; for such a system the restaurant train is provided with a special warning buzzer that indicates the moment of opening the doors for the entry or exit of the diners. This operation must be undertaken without obstructions of any kind, for which reason the restaurant guards act in synchronization with those at the station, forming in a split second a double row that frames the customers and, at the same time, prevents any johnny-come-lately, some innocent tourist or evil political provocateur, from sneaking into the restaurant car.

As is natural, thanks to the private advertisements of the establishment, the customers are informed of the fact that they should wait for the train at a precise spot on the platform, a sector that changes every two weeks in order to put off the common passengers, and which has as a secret clue one of the posters advertising cheese, detergents, or mineral water pasted on the platform walls. Although the system is expensive, the administration has preferred to give out information about these changes by means of a confidential bulletin rather than putting up an arrow or some other precise indicator in the necessary place, for many youthful drifters or the tramps who use the subway as a hotel wouldn't be long in gathering there, even if only to admire close-up the dazzling scene of the restaurant car, which, without doubt, would arouse their basest appetites.

The informative bulletin contains other equally necessary instructions for the customers. To wit: the latter must know the line the restaurant runs on for lunchtime and for dinner, and that the line is changed daily in order to spread out the diners' pleasant experiences. To that end there is a precise calendar that goes out with the indication of the chef's specials which are announced every fortnight, and even though the daily change in lines increases the management's difficulties in matters of getting on and off, it avoids the ordinary passengers' attention being concentrated, dangerously perhaps, on the two gastronomical periods of the day. Anyone who receives the bulletin can tell whether the restaurant will cover the stations that go from the Mairie de Montreuil to the Porte de Sèvres or will be on the line that links the Château de Vincennes and the Porte de Neuilly; added to the pleasure meant for the customers through visiting different stretches of subway routes and appreciating the not always nonexistent differences among stations is an important element of security in light of the unforeseeable reactions that might be provoked by a daily repeat appearance of the restaurant car at stations where there is a similar repetition of passengers.

Those who have eaten along any of the itineraries

agree that an additional delight of a refined table is a pleasant and sometimes useful sociological experience. Seated in such a way that they can enjoy a direct view through the windows facing the platform, the customers have an opportunity to witness in multiple forms, densities, and rhythms the spectacle of a hard-working people heading to their jobs or, at the end of the day, preparing themselves for a well-deserved rest, quite often falling asleep on their feet in anticipation on the platforms. In order to favor the spontaneity of these observations, management bulletins recommend to their customers that they not concentrate their looks on the platforms too much, for it would be preferable for them to do so between mouthfuls or at breaks in their conversation; it's obvious that excessive scientific curiosity might bring on some inopportune reaction, unjust of course, on the part of people culturally untutored for the understanding of the enviable mental latitude possessed by modern democracies. It is best particularly to avoid a prolonged ocular examination when groups of workers or students predominate on the platforms; the observation can be done without risk in the case of people who, by their age or dress, show a higher grade of possible relationship to the diners and even go so far as to wave at them and show that their presence on the train is reason for national pride or a positive symptom of progress.

During the last few weeks, as public knowledge of this new service has reached almost all urban sectors, a greater deployment of police can be noticed at stations visited by the restaurant car, which goes to prove the interest of official bodies in the maintenance of such an interesting innovation. The police can be seen to be particularly active in the movement of diners leaving, especially if it's the case of isolated people or couples; under those circumstances, once the directional double line formed by railroad and restaurant employees has been passed, a varying number of armed police graciously accompany the customers to the subway exit, where their car is generally waiting for them, since the customers have taken good care to organize the details of their pleasant gastronomic outings. These precautions have many explanations; at a time when the most irresponsible and unjustified violence has turned the New York subway into a jungle and the one in Paris too sometimes, the prudent foresight of the authorities deserves whole-hearted praise, not only from restaurant customers but also from passengers in general, who will no doubt give thanks for not seeing themselves dragged along by the obscure maneuvers of provocateurs or mental cases—almost always socialists or communists when not anarchists—and the list goes on and is longer than a poor man's hope.

Steady, Steady, Six Already

After the age of fifty we begin to die little by little in the deaths of others. The great magi, the shamans of our youth, successively go off. Sometimes we no longer thought much about them, they'd remained behind in history; *Other Voices, Other Rooms* summoned us. In some way they were still there, but like paintings no longer viewed as in the beginning, poems that only vaguely scent our memory.

Then—everyone has his beloved ghosts, his major interceders—the day arrives when the first of them horribly bursts out in the newspaper and radio scene. Maybe we'll take some time to realize that our death has begun on that day too; I knew it the night when in the middle of dinner someone indifferently alluded to a television news item that said Jean Cocteau had just died in Milly-la-Fôret and a piece of me fell dead too onto the tablecloth in the midst of the conversational phrases.

The rest have followed along, always in the same way, radio or newspaper, Louis Armstrong, Pablo

Picasso, Igor Stravinsky, Duke Ellington, and last night, while I was coughing in a hospital in Havana, last night in a friend's voice that brought the rumor from the outside world to my bed, Charles Chaplin. I shall leave this hospital, I shall leave cured, that's for certain, but, for a sixth time, a little less alive.

Dialogue of a Break

To be read in two voices, impossibly of course.

"It isn't as if we didn't know"

"Yes, especially that, not finding"

"But maybe we've been looking for it ever since the day when"

"Maybe not, and yet every morning that"

"Nothing but deception, the moment comes when you look at yourself like"

"Who can say, I still"

"It's not enough to want to, if, besides that, there's no proof of"

"You see, you can never be certain that"

"Certainly, each one of us is demanding evidence now in view of"

"As if kissing each other meant signing a release, as if looking at each other"

"Under the clothing there's no more waiting for the skin that"

"That's not the worst part of it, I sometimes

think; there's that other business, the words when"

"Or the silence, which in those days was worth"

"We knew enough to open the window as soon as"

"And that way of turning over the pillow looking for"

"Like a language of damp perfumes that"

"You'd keep on shouting while I"

"We'd fall into the same blind avalanche until"

"I was waiting to hear what always"

"And pretending to fall asleep in the midst of knotted sheets and sometimes"

"Between petting we'd insult the alarm clock that"

"But it was nice getting up and fighting over the"

"And the winner, all soaked, owner of the dry towel"

"Toast and coffee, the shopping list, and that"

"Everything's just the same, you might even say that"

"Exactly the same, except that instead"

"Like trying to tell a dream that after"

"Running a pencil over an outline, repeating by heart something that"

"Knowing at the same time how"

"Oh yes, but nearly hoping an encounter with"

"A little more marmalade and some"

"Thanks, I haven't got"

Sunset Hunter

If I were a moviemaker I'd set about hunting sunsets. I've got it all figured out except for the capital needed for the safari, because a sunset doesn't let itself be caught just like that, I mean that sometimes it starts out as a silly little thing and just when you abandon it, all of its feathers open up, or, just the opposite, it's a chromatic extravaganza and suddenly you're left with a kind of souped-up parrot, and in both cases you have to count on a camera with good color film, travel expenses and an itinerary of overnight stops, keeping watch on the sky, and the choice of the most propitious horizon, none of it cheap. In any case, I think that if I were a moviemaker I would set things up to hunt sunsets, just one sunset actually, but in order to arrive at the definitive sunset I'd have to film forty or fifty, because if I were a moviemaker I'd be just as demanding as with words, women, and geopoliticians.

That's not how it is and I console myself by imagining that the sunset has been caught already,

sleeping in its long canned spiral. My plan: not just
the hunting but the restitution of the sunset to my
fellows who don't know much about it, I mean city
people who watch the sun go down, if they happen
to see it, behind the post office, the apartment build-
ings across the way, or on a subhorizon of television
antennas and lampposts. The movie would be silent,
or with a soundtrack that would record only the
sounds contemporary to the filmed sunset, probably
some barking dog or the buzzing of horseflies, with
luck the little bell of a sheep, or the breaking of a
wave if it's a maritime sunset.

Through experience and a wristwatch I know that
a good sunset doesn't last more than twenty minutes
between climax and anticlimax, two things I would
eliminate in order to leave only its slow internal
play, its kaleidoscope of imperceptible mutations; it
would be one of those films they call documentaries,
shown before Brigitte Bardot while people are
settling down and looking at the screen as if they
were on a bus or a subway. My film would have a
printed explanation (maybe a voice-over) along
these lines: "What you are about to see is the sunset
of June 7, 1976, filmed in X with M film and fixed
camera, without interruption for Z minutes." The
audience will be informed that outside of the sunset absolutely nothing happens, for which reason
they are advised to carry on as if they were at home
and to do whatever they feel like doing, looking at

the sunset, for example, turning their backs on it, talking to others, strolling about, etc. We're terribly sorry that we can't suggest that they smoke, something that's always so beautiful at sunset, but the medieval conditions of movie theaters require, as everybody knows, the prohibition against that excellent habit. On the other hand, it's not forbidden to take a good swig from the pocket flask that the distributor of the film sells in the lobby.

It's impossible to predict the fate of my film; people go to the movies to forget about themselves, and a sunset leans exactly in the opposite direction, it's the moment when, perhaps, we see ourselves a little more naked, that happens to me, in any case, and it's painful and useful; maybe others can make use of it too, you never know.

Ways of Being Held Prisoner

It's always been just a matter of getting started and away we go. The first line I read of this text makes me bump into everything because I can't accept the fact that Gago is in love with Lil; in fact, I only learned it a few lines ahead but time is different here, you, for example, who are starting to read this page will find out that I don't agree and that way you'll learn in advance that Gago has fallen in love with Lil, but things aren't that way: you weren't here yet (or the text either) when Gago was already my lover; I'm not here either, since that isn't the theme of the text for now and I've got nothing to do with what's going to happen when Gago goes to the Libertad Theater to see a Bergman film and in between two cheap advertising trailers discovers Lil's legs beside his and in exactly the way Stendhal describes it, a glowing crystallization begins (Stendhal thinks it's progressive, but Gago). In other words, I reject this text where someone writes that I reject this text; I feel trapped, annoyed, betrayed, because I'm not even the one who's saying it but rather someone who's manipulating and regulating and coagulating me, I'd say that he's putting me on as well, it's clearly written: I'd say that he's putting me on as well.

He's putting you on too (you who are starting to read this page, that's how it's written above), and if that wasn't enough, Lil, who doesn't know not only that Gago is my lover but that Gago doesn't understand a thing about women, although in the Libertad, etc. How can I accept that when they leave they're talking now about Bergman and Liv Ullmann (they've both read Liv's memoirs and, of course, a theme for whiskey and great aesthetico-libidinous fraternizing, the drama of the actress mother who wants to be a mother and still be an actress with Bergman behind most of the time, a great son of a bitch on the paternal and marital plane): all of that goes on until a quarter after eight when Lil says I've got to go home, Mama's not feeling well, and Gago I'll take you, I've got my car parked on the Plaza Lavalle and Lil okay, you made me drink too much, Gago allow me, Lil of course, the warm firmness of the bare forearm (that's what it says, two adjectives, two nouns, just like that) and I've got to accept their getting into the Ford, which, among other qualities, has that of being mine, that Gago takes Lil to San Isidro, wasting my gas, with what it costs today, that Lil introduces him to her mother, arthritic but erudite as regards Francis Bacon, whiskey again and I'm sorry that you've got to go all the way back downtown, Lil, I'll think about you and the trip will be short, Gago, here's my phone number, Lil, oh thank you, Gago.

It's more than obvious that there's no way I can agree with things that try to modify the deepest reality; I persist in believing that Gago didn't go to the movies or meet Lil, even though the text tries to convince me and therefore put me into despair. Must I accept a text simply because it says that I must accept a text? I can, on the other hand, accept what one part of me considers a perfidious ambiguity (because probably yes; probably the movies) but at least the following phrases carry Gago downtown where he leaves the car improperly parked as always, comes up to my apartment knowing that I'm waiting for him at the end of this paragraph too long already as is all waiting for Gago, and after bathing and putting on the orange robe I gave him for his birthday he comes to lean against the divan where I'm reading with relief and love that Gago comes to lean against the divan where I'm reading with relief and love, perfumed and insidious is the Chivas Regal and the midnight Virginia tobacco, his curly hair where I softly sink my hand to bring out that first dreamy moan, without Lil or Bergman (what a delight to read it just like that, without Lil or Bergman) until that moment when very slowly I will begin to loosen the belt of the orange robe, my hand will run down Gago's smooth, warm chest, it will pass over the thickness of his stomach seeking the first spasm, entwined we will go off to the bedroom and fall onto the bed together, I will seek his throat where I like to nibble ever so softly and he'll murmur just a minute, will murmur wait just a minute I have to make a call. To Lil, of course, I got back okay, thanks, silence, then I'll see you tomorrow at eleven, silence, at eleven-thirty, all right, silence, for lunch of course, silly, silence, I said silly, silence, why so formal, silence, I don't know but it's like we've known each other for a long time, silence, you're a sheer delight, silence, and I as I put my robe on again and go back to the living room and the Chivas Regal, at least I've got that, the text says that at least I've got that, that I put my robe on again and go back to the living room, while Gago continues talking on the phone to Lil, it's useless to reread it to make sure, that's what it says, that I go back to the living room and the Chivas Regal while Gago continues talking on the phone to Lil.

The Direction of the Look

TO JOHN BARTH

In vaguely Ilium, perhaps in a Tuscan countryside at the end of Guelphs and Ghibellines and why not in lands of Danes or in that region of Brabant wetted by so many bloods: a mobile scene like the light that runs across the contest between two dark clouds, stripping bare and cloaking regiments and rear guards, face-to-face encounters with daggers or halberds, an anamorphic vision given only to one who will accept delirium and seek in the profile of the day its sharpest angle, its coagulum midst smoke and routs and oriflammes.

A battle, then, the usual waste that overflows senses and future chronicles. How many saw the hero at his highest hour, surrounded by scarlet foemen? Efficient machine of the poet or the bard: slowly, choosing and telling. Also the one who listens or the one who reads: attempting only to demultiply the vertigo. Then yes, perhaps, like one who detaches from the crowd the face that will cipher its life, Charlotte Corday's choice over the naked body of Marat, chest, belly, throat. Like that now amongst bonfires and countermands, in a whirl-wind of fleeing gonfalons or Achaean foot soldiers concentrating their advance against the obsessive base of the still unconquered walls: the roulette eye placing its ball in the number that will sink thirty-five hopes into nothingness so as to raise up one single red or black fate.

Inscribed in an instantaneous scene, the hero in slow motion draws his sword from a body still sustained by the air, looking at it with disdain in its bloody fall. Covering him, facing those who drive in on him, the shield throws into their faces shrapnel of light as the vibration of his hand makes the bronze images tremble. They will attack him, that is certain, but they will not cease to see what he shows them in one last challenge. Dazzled (the shield, a burning glass, roasts them in a fire of images aggravated by the sunset and the burning), they find it hard to separate the bronze relief from the ephemeral ghosts of the battle.

On the gilded mass the smith sought to represent himself at his forge, pounding the metal and taking pleasure in the concentric play of forging a shield that lifts its curved eyelid to show among so many figures (it shows it now to those who die or kill in the absurd contradiction of battle) the naked body of the hero in a clearing in the forest, embracing a woman who sinks a hand into his hair as if caressing or rejecting him. The bodies juxtaposed on the fight that the scene envelops with a slow outpouring of fronds (a stag between two trees, a bird fluttering over their heads) the lines of force would seem to be concentrated on the mirror held in the woman's other hand and in which her eyes, perhaps not wishing to see who is deflowering her like that among ash trees and ferns, will desperately seek the image that a slight movement locates and makes clear.

Kneeling beside a fountain, the youth has taken off his helmet and his dark curls fall down over his shoulders. He has already drunk and his lips are wet, drops of water fuzz; the lance lies to one side, resting after a long march. A new Narcissus, the youth looks at himself in the quivering clearness at his feet, but one might say that he only manages to see his enamored memory, the unattainable image of a woman lost in remote contemplation.

It is she again, her body of milk no longer intertwined with the one that opens her and penetrates, but gracefully exposed to the light of a large window at dusk, turned almost in profile toward a painting on an easel that the last rays of the sun lick with orange and amber. It might be said that his eyes can only manage to see the first plane of that painting where the artist represented himself, secret and detached. Neither he nor she looks toward the depth of the landscape where reclining bodies are glimpsed beside a fountain, the hero dead in battle under the shield that his hand clutches in one last challenge, and the youth, whom an arrow in flight has seemed to designate, multiplying to infinity the perspective that is resolved in the distance by a confusion of men in retreat and broken battle standards.

The shield no longer reflects the sun; its extinguished plate, which no longer looks bronze, contains the image of the blacksmith finishing the depiction of a battle and seeming to sign it at its most intense point with the figure of the hero surrounded by foemen plunging his sword into the chest of the nearest and to defend himself raising his bloody shield on which little can be seen amidst the fire and the rage and the vertigo, unless that naked image could be the woman's, that her body could be the one that surrenders without effort to the slow caresses of the youth who has rested his lance on the edge of a fountain.

III

"No, no. No crime," said Sherlock Holmes, laughing. "Only one of those whimsical little incidents which will happen when you have four million human beings all jostling each other within the space of a few square miles."

Sir Arthur Conan Doyle
The Blue Carbuncle

Lucas, His Wandering Songs

As a child he'd heard it on a scratchy record whose long-suffering Bakelite no longer could bear the weight of pickups with a mica diaphragm and a huge steel needle; Sir Harry Lauder's voice came as if from far away and that was how it had been, it had entered the record out of the mists of Scotland and now was emerging into the blinding summer of the Argentine pampas. The song was mechanical and routine, a mother saying goodbye to her son who was going far away and Sir Harry was not a very sentimental mother even though his metallic voice (almost all of them became that way after the recording process) managed to filter out a melancholy that by that time Lucas the child was already beginning to hang out with too much.

Twenty years later the radio brought him a piece of the song in the voice of the great Ethel Waters. The hard, irresistible hand of the past drove him out onto the street, shoved him into the Casa Iriberri record shop, and that night he listened to the record

and I think that he cried over a lot of things, alone
in his room and drunk with self-pity and Catamarca
grappa, which is notoriously lachrymogenous. He
wept without really knowing why he was weeping,
what obscure summons required it out of that ballad
that now, yes, now was bringing out all its meaning,
its maudlin beauty. In the voice of the one who
had conquered Buenos Aires with her version of
"Stormy Weather," the old song went back to prob-
able southern origins, rescued from the music-hall
triviality with which Sir Harry had sung it. Who
can say, after all, whether that ballad came from
Scotland or from Mississippi; now, in any case, it
was filled with blackness from the first words:

> So you're going to leave the old home, Jim,
> Today you're going away,
> You're going among the city folks to dwell.

Ethel Waters was saying goodbye to her son with
a premonitory vision of misfortune, redeemable only
by a return à la Peer Gynt, wings broken and all
pride drunken away. The oracle was seeking to hide
behind some *ifs* that had nothing to do with
Kipling's, some *ifs* of guilty fulfillment:

> If sickness overtakes you,
> If'n old companion shakes you,
> And through this world you wander all alone,

If friends you've got not any,
In your pockets not a penny—

If all that, Jim still had the key to the last door
left:

There's a mother always waiting
For you at home, old sweet home.

Naturally, Dr. Freud, the spider, and all that. But
music is a no-man's-land where it matters little
whether or not Turandot is frigid or Siegfried a pure
Aryan, complexes and myths are resolved in the
melody and so what, all that matters is a voice
murmuring the tribal words, the recurrence of what
we are, of what we're going to be:

And if you get in trouble, Jim,
Just write and let me know.

So easy, so beautiful, so Ethel Waters. *Just write,*
of course. The problem is the envelope. What
name, what address, to put on the envelope, Jim.

Lucas, His Modesty

In today's apartments, as is well known, the guest goes to the bathroom and the others keep on talking about Biafra and Michel Foucault, but there is something in the air as if everybody wanted to forget that he has hearing and at the same time ears are attuned toward the sacred place that in our huddled society is, naturally, scarcely ten feet away from the place where those high-level conversations are taking place, and it is certain that in spite of all efforts the absent guest will make not to reveal his activities and those of his fellows to raise the volume of the dialogue, at some moment there will reverberate one of those dull sounds that let themselves be heard under the least indicated circumstances, or, in the best of cases, the pathetic tearing of cheap toilet paper as a piece is ripped off the pink or green roll.

If the guest who has gone to the bathroom is Lucas, his horror can only be compared to the intensity of the colic that has obliged him to shut himself up in the ominous redoubt. In that horror there is neither neurosis nor any complex but the certainty of a recurrent intestinal behavior, that is to say, everything will start off fine, softly and silently, but then toward the end, keeping the same relationship between powder and bird-shot in a hunting cartridge, a rather horrendous detonation will shake the toothbrushes in their racks and agitate the plastic shower curtain.

Lucas can do nothing to avoid it; he has tried all methods, such as leaning over to touch the floor with his head, leaning backward to the point where his feet brush against the wall opposite, turning sidewise, and, as an extreme measure, grasping his buttocks and separating them as much as possible so as to increase the diameter of the tempestuous conduit. Vain is the addition of such silencing devices as placing about his thighs all the towels within reach and even his hosts' bathrobes; practically always, at the end of what could have been an agreeable transfer, the final fart bursts forth tumultuously.

When it is someone else's turn to go to the bathroom, Lucas trembles for him, for he is certain that at any second the first yoicks of ignominy will resound; it surprises him a little that people don't seem to worry too much about things like that, although it's obvious that they're not unaware of what's going on and even cover it up with the noise of spoons in cups and the totally unnecessary movement of armchairs. When nothing happens, Lucas is happy and immediately asks for another cognac, by which he gives himself away so that everybody realizes he had been tense and anxious while Mrs. Broggi took care of her necessities. How different, Lucas thinks, from the simplicity of children who come into the most elegant of gatherings and announce: Mama, I have to make poopy. How happy, Lucas continues thinking, is that anonymous poet who composed the quatrain that proclaims that there is no pleasure so exquisite / as that derived from a good, slow shit, / nor pleasure as delicate as that / which comes on after one has shat. In order to rise to that gentleman's heights, one would have to be exempt from all danger of intemperate or tempestuous windiness, unless the bathroom in the house was upstairs or was one of those little tin-roofed privies separated from the ranch house by a goodly distance.

Having entered poetic territory now, Lucas remembers the line from Dante where each devil *avea del cul fatto trombetta*, and with that mental reference to highest culture he considers himself somewhat blameless for meditations that have little to do with what Dr. Berenstein is saying with regard to housing laws.

Lucas, His Studies on a
Society of Consumers

Since progress knows-no-limits, in Spain they sell packages that contain thirty-two boxes of matches (tapers, as they say), each of which displays the gaudy reproduction of a complete chess set.

Very swiftly, a wise gentleman put on the market a chess set whose thirty-two pieces can serve as coffee cups; almost immediately the Bazar Dos Mundos turned out coffee cups that allow rather flabby ladies a variety of sufficiently rigid bras, after which Yves Saint Laurent has just brought out a bra in which two soft-boiled eggs can be served in a most suggestive manner.

What a pity that up till now no one has found a different application for soft-boiled eggs, a thing that disheartens those who eat them between great sighs; that's the way certain chains of happiness are broken and remain only in chains and quite dear, it might be said in passing.

Lucas, His Friends

The list of cronies is large and varied, but who can say why it occurs to him now to think especially about the Cedróns, and thinking about the Cedróns means so many things that he doesn't know where to begin. The only thing in Lucas's favor is that he doesn't know all of the Cedróns, only three of them, but who can say whether or not that's in his favor in the end. He's been given to understand that the brothers add up to a sum of six or nine, in any case, he knows three, so hang on, we're off and running.

These three Cedróns consist of the musician Tata, Jorge the filmmaker, and Alberto the painter. Trying to separate them is something else again, but when they decide to get together and they invite you for some meat tarts, then they really are death in three volumes.

What can I tell you about getting there, from the street you can hear a kind of uproar on one of the upper floors, and if you pass one of their Parisian neighbors you can see on their faces that corpselike paleness of people who have witnessed a phenomenon that goes beyond the parameters of that strait-laced and muffed race. No need to ask what floor the Cedróns are on because the noise guides you up the stairs to one of the doors that looks less door than the others and also gives the impression of being red-hot because of what's going on inside, to the point that you'd better not knock too long because you'll scorch your knuckles. Of course, the door is most likely wide open, since the Cedróns are also going in and out and, besides, why close a door that gives such good ventilation from the stairway.

What happens as you enter renders coherent description impossible, because as soon as you cross the threshold there's a little girl who grabs you by the knees and covers your topcoat with spittle, and at the same time a little boy who has climbed up onto the bookcase in the foyer dives at your neck like a kamikaze, so that if you had the vague idea of coming with a bottle of cheap red, the instantaneous result is a gaudy puddle on the carpet. This doesn't bother anyone, of course, because at that same moment the wives of the Cedróns appear from different rooms, and while one of them untangles you from the kids on top of you, the others sop up the unfortunate burgundy with some rags that probably go back to the times of the Crusades. With all this, Jorge has told you in detail the plots of two or three novels that he intends to film, Alberto holds back two other children armed with bows and arrows and, what is worse, endowed with singular marksmanship, and Tata comes out of the kitchen wearing an apron that once knew the color white in its earliest days and which envelops him majestically from the armpits down, giving him a surprising resemblance to Mark Antony or any of the types who vegetate in the Louvre or work at being statues in parks. The great news proclaimed simultaneously by ten or twelve voices is that there are meat tarts, into the making of which went the participation of Tata's wife and Tata himself, but whose recipe has been considerably improved by Alberto, who is of the opinion that leaving Tata and his wife alone in the kitchen can only lead to the worst of catastrophes. As for Jorge, who for no reason will refuse to stay out of what is coming, he has already brought forth generous quantities of wine and everybody, once these tumultuous pre- liminaries have been resolved, settles onto the bed, onto the floor, or where there isn't a kid crying or peeing, which ends up as the same thing but at different levels.

A night with the Cedróns and their unselfish ladies (I say unselfish because if I were a woman and also the woman of one of the Cedróns, it would have been a long time back that the bread knife would have put a voluntary end to my suffering, but they not only don't suffer but are even worse than the Cedróns, something that delights me because it's good for someone to get the best of them from time to time, and I think the women get the best of them all the time), a night with the Cedróns is a kind of South American summary that explains and justifies the stupefied wonder with which Europeans attend to their music, their literature, their painting, and their movies or theatre. Now that I think of it, I remember something told me by the Quilapayúns, who are cronopios just as mad as the Cedróns, but musicians all, the question being whether for better or for worse. During a trip through Germany (the eastern one but I think the effects of the case would have been the same no matter which) the Quilapayúns decided to have an outdoor barbecue Chilean style, but to their general surprise they discovered that in that country you can't have a picnic in the woods without permission from the authorities. Permission isn't hard to get, one has to admit, and the police took it so seriously that at the time for lighting the fires and placing the creatures on their respective spits, a fire truck appeared, whose passengers spread out through the nearby woods and spent five hours making sure that the fire wouldn't spread through the Wagnerian firs and other plants that abound in Teutonic forests. If memory serves, several of those firemen ended up stuffing their guts, as befits the prestige of their calling, and that day there was a fraternizing that is unusual between those in uniform and civilians. It's true that the fireman's uniform is the least whorish of all uniforms, and on the day when with the help of millions of Quilapayúns and Cedróns we consign all South American uniforms to the trash can, the only ones saved will be firemen's and we'll even invent more handsome models for them so the lads will be happy while they put out fires or save poor ravished girls who have decided to jump in the river for want of something better.

With all this the meat tarts disappear with a speed worthy of people who look at each other with a fierce hatred because this fellow had seven and the other only five and at one of these points the coming and going of platters ceases and some poor fool suggests coffee, as if that were food. The ones who always seem the least interested are the kids, whose number will still be an enigma for Lucas, for as soon as one disappears behind a bed or into the hallway, two others burst out of a closet or slide down the trunk of a rubber plant until they sit smack in a platter full of meat tarts. These tots feign a certain disdain for such a noble Argentine product, under the pretext that their respective mothers have already nourished them as a precaution a half hour before, but judging from the way in which the meat tarts disappear, one can only be convinced that they're an important element in infantile metabolism, and that if Herod were there that night another cock would have crowed for us and Lucas, instead of twelve meat tarts, would have been able to eat seventeen, all, of course, with the necessary breaks for trips to the wine cellar for a couple of quarts, which, as is well known, settle protein.

Above, below, and in the midst of the meat tarts there reigns a clamor of declarations, questions, protests, laughs, and general displays of joy and love that creates an atmosphere alongside which a war council to Tehuelche or Mapuche Indians would resemble the wake for a law professor. From time to time raps can be heard on the ceiling, on the floor, and on the two adjoining walls, and almost always it is Tata (tenant of the apartment) who announces that it's only the neighbors, which doesn't make for the least cause for worry. The fact that it's one in the morning is no reason for aggrievement or anything else, because at two thirty when we go downstairs four steps at a time singing the tango lines *que te abrás en las paradas / con cafishos milongueros* at the top of our lungs. There has already been sufficient time to solve most of the problems of the planet, we've agreed to screw more than four people who deserve it and how, date books have been filled with telephone numbers and addresses and get-togethers in cafés and other apartments, and tomorrow the Cedróns are going to split up because

Alberto is going back to Rome, Tata is leaving with
his quartet to sing in Poitiers, and Jorge is splitting
for God knows where but always with his light
meter in his hand and no holding him. It isn't of
no use to add that Lucas goes home with the feeling
that on his shoulders he has a sort of pumpkin
filled with horseflies, Boeing 707s, and several super-
imposed solos by Max Roach. But what does he care
about a hangover if down below there's some little
hot thing that must be the meat tarts, and between
down and up there's something even warmer still,
a heart that repeats what fuckups, what fuckups,
what glorious fuckups, what irreplaceable fuckups,
crazy motherfuckers.

Lucas, His Shoeshines 1940

Lucas in the shoeshine parlor off the Plaza de Mayo, put black polish on my left shoe and yellow polish on the right one. What? Black here and yellow here. But sir. Here's where you put the black, kid, and that's enough, I've got to concentrate on the racing form.

Things like that are never easy, it doesn't seem like much but it's almost like Copernicus or Galileo, those shakes at the base of the tree that leave everyone flat on his back looking up. This time, for example, there's the loudmouth of the day who from the back of the room tells the man next to him that you never know what fairies are going to think of next, eh, then Lucas draws himself away from a possible pick in the fourth race (Paladino up) and almost sweetly seeks the advice of the bootblack: the kick in the ass, shall I give it to him with the yellow one or the black one?

The bootblack doesn't know which shoe to recommend, he's finished the black one and can't make up his mind, really can't make up his mind to begin on the other one. Yellow, reflects Lucas aloud, and at the same time it's a command, the yellow one is better because it's a dynamic color, it makes an entry, you, there, what are you waiting for. Yes sir right away. The one in back has started getting up to come to investigate that kick business, but Deputy Poliyatti, who isn't president of the *Unione e Benevolenza* Club for nothing, lets his fiery elocution be heard, gentlemen, don't make waves, we've got enough problems with the isobars, it's incredible how one sweats in this metropolis, the incident is of no account and there's nothing that can be written about taste, apart from the fact that the police station is across the way there and the fuzz is hyperesthetic after the last protest meeting of the youth, as those of us who have long since left behind the stormy weather of the first period of existence say. That's right, Doctor, approves one of the deputy's toadies, no rough stuff here. He insulted me, the one in back says, I was only talking about fags in general. Worse yet, says Lucas, in any case I'm going to be over there on the corner for the next fifteen minutes. That's funny, says the one in back, right in front of the precinct. Naturally, says Lucas, let's see if on top of a faggot you're going to take me for a boob. Gentlemen, proclaims Deputy Poliyatti, this episode belongs to history now, there's no reason for a duel, please don't oblige me to use my authority and things like that. That's right, Doctor, says the toady.

Upon which Lucas goes out onto the street and his shoes gleam like a sunflower on the right and Oscar Peterson on the left. No one comes looking for him when the fifteen minutes are up, something that produces a not insignificant relief in him, which he immediately celebrates with a beer and a dark cigarette, a matter of maintaining the chromatic symmetry.

Lucas, His Birthday Presents

It would be too easy just buying a cake at the bakery called The Two Chinese; even Gladis would realize it, in spite of the fact that she's a little nearsighted, and Lucas decides that it's well worth the trouble of spending half a day personally preparing a gift whose recipient deserves that and much more but at least that. Since morning now he's gone up and down the neighborhood buying wheat flour and cane sugar, then he attentively reads the recipe for the Five-Star cake, the crowning glory of Doña Gertrudis, big mama of all fine tables, and the kitchen in his apartment in a short time is transformed into a kind of laboratory of Dr. Mabuse. The friends who come by to discuss hippic prognostications don't take long to leave as they feel the first symptoms of asphyxia, as Lucas sifts, strains, blends, and powders the diverse and delicate ingredients with such passion that the air tends not to lend itself too much to its usual functions.

Lucas has some experience in the matter and, furthermore, the cake is for Gladis, which means several layers of flaky pastry (it's not easy to make a good flaky pastry) between which exquisite confections are placed, the skins of Venezuelan almonds, shredded coconut, not only shredded but ground to the point of atomic disintegration in an obsidian mortar; to this is added the outer decorations, modulated on Raúl Soldi's palette but with arabesques inspired to a large degree by Jackson Pollock, except for the most austere part, dedicated to the inscription JUST FOR YOU, whose almost overwhelming relief is provided by preserved cherries and orange slices and which Lucas sets in 14-point Baskerville, which adds an almost solemn note to the dedication.

Carrying the Five-Star Cake on a platter or plate seems to Lucas to be of a vulgarity worthy of a dinner at the Jockey Club, so he installs it delicately onto a white cardboard tray whose size is barely greater than that of the cake. At party time he puts on his pinstriped suit and crosses the foyer full of guests carrying the tray with the cake in his right hand, a feat notable in itself, while with his left hand he gently moves aside the marveling relatives and more than four gate-crashers who right there swear to die like heroes before missing out on the enjoyment of that splendid gift. For that reason a kind of cortege is immediately organized behind Lucas in which shouts, applause, and borborigmies of propitiatory saliva abound, and the entry of all into the living room is not far removed from a provincial version of *Aida*. Understanding the gravity of the moment, Gladis's parents join hands in a rather well-known but always well-received gesture, and the one receiving the homage quickly breaks off an insignificant conversation to come forward with all her teeth in the front row and her eyes looking at the ceiling. Happy, in the heights, feeling that so many hours of work are culminating in something that approaches apotheosis, Lucas essays the final gesture of the Great Work: his hand rises in the offertory of the cake, he tilts it dangerously in full view of public anxiety, and he mashes it full into Gladis's face. All of this scarcely takes more time than Lucas takes in recognizing the pavement of the street, enveloped in a rain of kicks that outdoes the Flood.

Lucas, His Working Methods

Since he sometimes can't sleep, instead of counting sheep he mentally answers the correspondence he's behind on, because his guilty conscience has as much insomnia as he. The courtesy letters, those of passion, intellectual ones, one by one he answers them with his eyes closed and with great discoveries of style and showy structures that please him because of their spontaneity and effectiveness, which naturally increases his insomnia. When he falls asleep all his correspondence has been brought up to date.

In the morning, of course, he's undone, and to make matters worse he has to sit down and write all the letters thought up during the night, which letters come out much worse, cold or clumsy or idiotic, meaning that tonight, too, he won't be able to sleep because of an excess of fatigue, apart from the fact that in the meantime new courtesy letters, those of passion, or intellectual ones have arrived and that Lucas, instead of counting sheep, will set about answering them with such perfection and elegance that Madame de Sévigné would have loathed him minutely.

Lucas, His Partisan Arguments

It almost always starts the same way, a notable political agreement in a lot of things and great mutual trust, but at some moment the nonliterary militants address the literary militants in a friendly way and bring up for the archi-nth time the matter of the message, the content intelligible for the greatest number of readers (or listeners or spectators, but especially readers, oh yes).

In those cases Lucas tends to be quiet, for his little books speak gaudily for him, but since they sometimes attack more or less fraternally and it's well known that there's no worse a punch than one thrown by your brother, Lucas puts on a laxative face and makes an effort to say things like the ones that follow, to wit:

"Comrades, the question will never be brought up
by writers who understand and live their task
like figureheads, out front
in the ship's course, receiving
all the wind and the salt of the foam. Period.
And it won't be brought up

because being a writer
$$\begin{cases} \text{poet} \\ \text{novelist} \\ \text{narrator} \end{cases}$$

that is, fictionant, imaginant, delirant,
mythopoietic, oracle or call him as you choose,
means in the firstest place
that language is a medium, as always,
but this medium is more than medium,
it's three-quarters at least.
Abbreviating two volumes and an appendix,
what you people ask of

the writer
$$\begin{cases} \text{poet} \\ \text{narrator} \\ \text{novelist} \end{cases}$$

is to give up going forward
and settle in the hic et nunc (translate, López!)
so his message doesn't go beyond
the spheres, semantical, syntactical,
cognoscitival, parametrical,
of circumstantial man. Ahem.
Said in other words, to abstain
from exploring beyond the explored,
or exploring by explaining the explored
so all exploration is integrated
into explorations that are done.
I shall tell you in confidence
would that there could
be reins in the race
for the head that's ahead. (That one's a gem.)
But there are scientific laws that deny

the possibility of such contradictory effort,
and there is something else, simple and grave:
there are no known limits to the imagination
except those of the word,
language and invention are fraternal enemies
and from that struggle literature is born,
the dialectical encounter of muse with scribe,
the unsayable seeking its word,
the word refusing to say it
until we wring its neck
and the scribe and the muse come together
at that rare instant that later on
we will call Vallejo or Mayakovsky."

A rather cavernous silence follows.

"That's fine," someone says, "but in the face of
the historical moment the writer and the artist, unless they're pure Ivorytower, have the duty, hear
me well, the duty to project their message on a
level of the broadest reception." Applause.

"I've always thought," Lucas observes modestly,
"that the writers you're alluding to are in the great
majority, a reason for which I am surprised at this
insistence on transforming a great majority into a
unanimity. Shit, what are you people so afraid of?
And who except the resentful and the mistrusting
can be bothered by experiences, let's call them
extreme and therefore difficult (difficult *first of all*
for the writer, and only afterwards for the public,
that must be stressed) when it's obvious that only a

few are carrying them forward? Couldn't it be, then, that for certain levels everything that isn't immediately clear is guiltily obscure? Can't there be a secret and sometimes sinister necessity to make the scale of values uniform so as to be able to stick your head up above the wave? Good lord, all these questions."

"There's only one answer," says a member of the group, "and it's this: The clear tends to be difficult to attain, for which reason the difficult tends to be a stratagem to disguise the difficulty of being easy." (Delayed ovation.)

"And we will go on for years and more years," moans Lucas,
"and always return to the same spot
since this is a matter
full of disillusionment." (Weak approval.)
"Because nobody will be able, except for the poet
    and he only sometimes,
to enter the wrestling match with the blank page
where everything is risked in the mystery
of unheeded laws, if they are laws,
of strange copulations between rhythm and meaning,
of ultima Thules in the middle of the strophe or
    story.
We will never be able to defend ourselves
because we know nothing of this vague knowledge,
of this quirk of fate that leads us
to swim under things, to climb up an adverb
that opens up a territory, one hundred new islands,

buccaneers with Remington or pen
attacking verbs or simple sentences
or receiving full in the face the wind
of a noun that contains an eagle."

"Or let it be, to simplify things," concludes
Lucas, as fed up as his comrades, "I propose, let's
say, a pact."

"No deals," roars the usual one in cases like this.

"A pact, nothing else. For you people, the
primum vivere, deinde philosophare is concentrated
in the historical *vivere*, which is fine and probably
is the only way to prepare the terrain for the
philosophizing and fictionizing and poetizing of the
future. But I aspire to suppress the divergence that
afflicts us, and, therefore, the pact consists of the
fact that you and we should at the same time abandon our most extreme conquests with an aim to
having our contact with our neighbor reach its
broadest radius. If we renounce verbal creation at
its dizziest and most rarefied level, you will renounce
science and technology in their equally dizzy and
rarefied forms, computers and jet aircraft, for example. If you deny us our poetical advance, why
should you sit back and enjoy scientific advance-
ment?"

"You're completely nuts," one with glasses says.

"Of course," Lucas concedes, "but you must see
how much fun I'm having. Come on, accept.

We'll write more simply (I'm just saying that because we really won't be able to), and you people
stop television (something you won't be able to do
either). We'll go to what's directly communicable,
and you people will give up cars and tractors and
pick up a shovel to plant potatoes. Do you realize
what that double turning back to the simple would
be, to what everybody understands, to communion
with nature without intermediaries?"

"I propose immediate defenestration upon a
unanimous vote," says a comrade who has opted to
break up with laughter.

"I vote no," says Lucas, who is already stroking
the glass of beer that always arrives just in time in
cases like these.

Lucas, His Traumatotherapies

Lucas was once operated on for appendicitis, and since the surgeon was a slob the wound became infected and it all went very poorly because in addition to the suppuration in radiant Technicolor, Lucas felt more flattened out than a dried fig. At that moment Dora and Celestino come in and tell him we're off to London right away, come spend a week with us, I can't, moans Lucas, it happens that, bah, I can change your bandages, says Dora, we'll buy some hydrogen peroxide and Band-Aids on the way, so in the end they take the train and the ferry and Lucas feels he's going to die because even though the wound doesn't hurt at all since it's barely an inch across, just the same he imagines what's going on beneath his pants and undershorts, when they finally get to the hotel and he takes a look at himself, it turns out that there's neither more nor less suppuration than in the hospital, and then Celestino says you see, and on the other hand here you'll have Turner's paintings, Laurence Olivier, and the steak and kidney pies that are the joy of my life.

The next day after having walked miles, Lucas is completely healed. Dora still puts on two or three Band-Aids for the pure pleasure of pulling out his hairs, and from that day on Lucas feels that he's discovered the traumatotherapy that, as can be seen, consists in doing exactly the opposite of what has been prescribed by Aesculapius, Hippocrates, and Dr. Fleming.

On numerous occasions Lucas, who has a good heart, has put his method into practice with surprising results among family and friends. For example, when his Aunt Angustias contracted a life-size cold and spent days and nights sneezing out of a nose that was looking more and more like that of a platypus, Lucas disguised himself as Frankenstein's monster and waited for her with a cadaverous smile behind a door. After giving out with a hair-raising shriek, Aunt Angustias fell into a faint on the cushions that Lucas had prepared in advance, and when the relatives roused her out of her swoon, the aunt was too busy telling what had happened to remember to sneeze, apart from the fact that for several hours she and the rest of the family could only think about chasing Lucas armed with sticks and bicycle chains. When Dr. Feta brought about a truce and they all gathered together to comment on the events and have a beer, Lucas made the casual observation that the aunt was completely cured of her cold, to which and with the habitual lack of logic in such cases the aunt answered him that that was no reason for her nephew to carry on like a son of a bitch.

Things like that dismay Lucas, but from time to time he applies his infallible system to himself or tries it out on others, and so when Don Crespo announces that his liver is bothering him, a diagnosis always accompanied by a hand holding up his guts and eyes like Bernini's Saint Teresa, Lucas fixes it so that his mother calls for cabbage stew with sausages and fatback, which Don Crespo loves almost more than a game of blackjack, and by the third helping it can be seen already that the invalid is interested in life and its merry games again, after which Lucas invites him to celebrate with some Catamarca grappa to settle the fat. When the family gets wind of these things there's an attempt at lynching, but deep down they begin to respect the traumatotherapy, which they call totherapy or traumatopy, it's all the same to them.

Lucas, His Dreams

Sometimes he suspects in them a concentric strategy of leopards who gradually approach a center, a quivering and crouching beast, the reason for the dream. But he awakes before the leopards reach their prey and all he has left is the smell of jungle and hunger and claws; with only that, he has to imagine the beast and that's impossible. He understands that the hunt can last through many other dreams, but the reason for that stealthy dilation, that endless approach, escapes him. Doesn't the dream have a motive and isn't the beast that motive? What does it mean by repeatedly hiding its possible name: sex, mother, stature, incest, stuttering, sodomy? Why, if that's what the dream is for, to reveal the beast in the end? But no, then the dream is to let the leopards continue their endless spiral and leave him only a glimpse of a clearing in the jungle, a squatting form, a stagnating smell. Its inefficacy is a punishment, perhaps a foretaste of hell; he will never come to know if the beast will tear the leopards to shreds, if it will rise up roaring with the knitting needles of the aunt who gave him that strange caress as she washed his thighs, one afternoon in the country place, back there in the twenties.

Lucas, His Hospital (II)

A vertigo, a sudden unreality. That's when the other, the unknown, the disguised reality, leaps like a toad into the middle of his face, let's say in the middle of the street (but what street?) one August morning in Marseilles. Easy, Lucas, let's take it piece by piece, you can't tell anything in a coherent way like that. Yes, but. *Coherent.* Well, okay, but let's try to grab the thread by the end, it so happens that you usually enter hospitals as a patient, but you can also do so in the capacity of an escort, which is what happened to you three days ago and more precisely during the early morning hours of the day before yesterday when an ambulance brought Sandra and you with her, you with your hand on hers, you looking at her unconscious and delirious, you with just enough time to toss four or five items, all wrong and useless, into a bag, you wearing what is so little August-in-Provence, shirt and pants and rope sandals, you resolving in an hour the business of the hospital and the ambulance and Sandra saying no and the doctor

with the tranquilizing injection, suddenly the friends
in your little village in the hills helping the stretcher
bearers get Sandra into the ambulance, vague
arrangements for tomorrow, telephone calls, best of
luck, the twin white doors closing capsule or crypt
and Sandra on the stretcher softly delirious and you
bouncing as you stand beside her because the ambulance has to go down a driveway of broken stones
until it gets to the road, midnight with Sandra and
two orderlies and a light that's already hospital,
tubes and bottles and the smell of an ambulance
lost in the hills until it reaches the highway, snorting
as if working up steam and taking off at full speed
with the two-note sound of its siren, the same one
heard so many times from outside an ambulance
and always with the same tightening of the stomach,
the same rejection.

You know the route, of course, but Marseilles
enormous and the hospital on the outskirts, two
nights without sleep are no help in understanding
the curves and approaches, the ambulance a white
box without windows, only Sandra and the orderlies
and you for almost two hours until an entrance,
formalities, signatures, bed, intern, check for the
ambulance, tips, all in an almost pleasant mist, a
friendly stupor now that Sandra is sleeping and
you're going to sleep too, the nurse has brought you
an extending chair, a thing whose mere sight gives
an idea of what kind of dreams will be had in it,

neither horizontal nor vertical, dreams with an oblique trajectory, punished kidneys, feet hanging in the air. But Sandra is sleeping and therefore all is well, Lucas smokes another cigarette and, surprisingly, the chair seems almost comfortable to him and we're already into the morning of the day before yesterday, room 303 with a large window that opens onto distant mountain ranges and parking lots too nearby where slow-moving workers go about among pipes and trucks and garbage cans, all things necessary to perk up the spirits of Sandra and Lucas.

All goes well because Sandra wakes up feeling better and more lucid, Lucas jokes with her and the interns and the professor and the nurses come and everything that must happen in a hospital in the morning happens, the hope of leaving right away to go back to the hills and rest, yogurt and mineral water, thermometer, blood pressure, more papers to sign in the office and that's when Lucas, who's gone down to sign those papers and gets lost on the way back and can't find the hallways or the elevators, has the first and still weak sensation of the toad in the middle of his face, it doesn't last long because everything is fine, Sandra hasn't left her bed and asks him to go out and buy her some cigarettes (a good sign) and to telephone their friends so that they'll know everything is going well and how quickly Sandra is going to return with Lucas to fields and calm and countryside says yes my love, of course, although he knows that the business of quickly is not going to be so quick, looks for the money he luckily remembered to bring, jots down the phone numbers and then Sandra tells him that she has no toothpaste (a good sign) or towels because in French hospitals you have to bring your own towels and soap and sometimes your silverware, then Lucas makes a list of hygienic purchases and adds a change of shirt for himself and another pair of shorts and for Sandra a nightgown and some sandals because they'd carried Sandra out barefoot, of course, to put her into the ambulance and who'd think about things like that at midnight when they've gone two nights without any sleep.

This time Lucas sees on the first try that the route to the exit isn't that difficult, elevator to the ground floor, a temporary passageway of planks and bare earth (they're modernizing the hospital and you have to follow the arrows that mark the passageways although sometimes they don't mark them or they mark them in two different directions), after a very long passage, really and truly, let's say the titular passage, with infinite rooms and offices on both sides, consultation rooms and radiology, stretchers with stretcher bearers and patients or only stretcher bearers or only patients, a turn to the left and another passageway with everything already described and much more, a narrow hallway that opens onto a crossway and finally the final hallway that leads to the exit. It's ten in the morning and Lucas a little somnambulistically asks the lady at Information how he can get the items on the list and the lady tells him that he has to go out of the hospital to the left or to the right, it doesn't matter, and you'll finally come to the commercial districts and of course nothing is very close because the hospital is enormous and functions in an ex-centric district, a description that Lucas would have found perfect if he hadn't been so blown, so far out, so still in the other context there in the hills, so there goes Lucas in his lounging slippers and his shirt wrinkled by the fingers of the night in the chair of supposed repose, he makes a mistake in direction and ends up in another wing of the hospital, retraces the inner streets, and finally comes to an exit door, all well up to that point, although from time to time a little of the toad in the face, but he clutches the mental wire that links him to Sandra up above there in that now invisible ward and it makes him feel good to think that Sandra is a little better, that he's bringing her a nightgown (if he can find one) and tooth-paste and sandals. Going down the street following the hospital wall that stonily reminds him of that of a cemetery, a heat that has driven everyone away, *there's no one*, only cars brushing him as they pass because the street is narrow, without trees or shade, the hour of the zenith so praised by the poet and which is squashing Lucas a little, discouraged and lost, hoping to see a supermarket finally or two or three shops at least, but nothing, more than a quarter of a mile to discover finally after a turn that Mammon is not dead, a service station, that's something at least, a store (closed), and farther on a supermarket with basketed old ladies leaving and entering and shopping carts and parking lots full of cars. There Lucas browses through the different sections, finds soap and toothpaste, but fails in all the rest, he can't go back to Sandra without the towel and the nightgown, he asks the cashier, who tells him to turn right then left (it isn't exactly left but almost) and the avenue Michelet where there's a big supermarket with towels and things like that. It all sounds like a bad dream because Lucas is about to drop from fatigue and the heat is unbearable and it's not a place where there are taxis and every new instruction takes him farther away from the hospital. We shall overcome, Lucas tells himself, mopping his face, it's certain that it's all a bad dream, Sandra teddy bear, but we shall overcome, you'll see, you'll get your towel and your nightgown and your sandals, whoreborn stuff.

Two or three times he stops to mop his face, that sweat isn't natural, it's something like fear, an absurd abandonment in the middle (or at the end) of a populous urban area, the second in France, it's something like a toad suddenly falling between your eyes, he no longer really knows where he is (he's in Marseilles but where, and that *where* isn't the place where he is, either), everything seems ridiculous and absurd and high noon, then a lady tells him oh the supermarket, go that way, then turn right and go to the boulevard, across the way is the Le Corbusier and right after that the supermarket, nightgowns, of course, certainly, mine for example, you're quite welcome, remember first that way and then turn.

Lucas's slippers are burning, his pants are nothing but a lump, not to mention his undershorts, which seem to have become subcutaneous, first that way and then turn and suddenly the Cité Radieuse, suddenly and soddenly he's facing a boulevard with trees and there opposite the famous Le Corbusier building that twenty years before he had visited between two legs of a trip through the south, except that then behind the radiant building there had been no supermarket and behind Lucas there had been no extra twenty years. Nothing of that really matters because the radiant building is just as beaten and as little radiant as the first time he saw it. The fact that he's passing under the belly of the immense animal of reinforced concrete to get to the nightgowns and towels isn't what matters now. It isn't that, but it happens there in any case, precisely in the only place familiar to Lucas inside that Marseillean periphery to which he has come not knowing how, a kind of parachutist jumping at two o'clock in the morning into unknown territory, into a hospital labyrinth, into an advance and an advance across instructions and streets empty of people, the only pedestrian among automobiles that are like indifferent meteors, and there beneath the concrete belly and legs of the only thing he knows, reknown in the unknown, it's there that the toad really lands in the middle of his face, a vertigo, a sudden unreality, and it's then that the other, the unknown, the disguised reality, opens up for a second like a cleft in the magma surrounding him. Lucas sees spells, trembles, smells the truth, to be lost and sweating far from the pillars, the braces, the known, the familiar, the house in the hills, the kitchen frills, the delightful routines, far even from Sandra who is so near but where because now he'll have to ask how to get back again, he'll never find a taxi in that hostile zone and Sandra isn't Sandra, she's a little wounded animal in a hospital bed but precisely yes, that's Sandra, that sweat and that anguish are sweat and anguish, Sandra is there nearby amidst uncertainty and vomiting, and the ultimate reality, the open cleft in the lie is being lost in Marseilles with Sandra sick and not happiness with Sandra in the house in the hills.

Naturally, that reality won't last, luckily, naturally Lucas and Sandra will leave the hospital, Lucas will forget this moment when alone and lost he finds himself in the absurd position of not being either alone or lost and yet, yet. He thinks vaguely (he feels better, he begins to make fun of those puerile thoughts) about a story read centuries ago, the story about a fake band in a Buenos Aires movie theater. There must have been some similarity between the guy who thought up that story and him, who can say, in any case Lucas shrugs his shoulders (really he does) and ends up finding the nightgown and the sandals, a pity there aren't any espadrilles for him, something unheard of and even scandalous in a proper high-noon city.

Lucas, His Pianists

Long is the list, as the keyboard is long, black and white, ivory and mahogany; a life of tones and semitones, of heavy and soft pedals. Like the kitten on the keys, the vulgar delight of the thirties, his memory is based on a bit of chance and the music jumps from here to there, remote yesterdays and todays from this morning (so certain because Lucas writes while a pianist plays for him from a record that creaks and gurgles as if it were hard for him to cover forty years, to throw out into the still unborn air the day when he recorded "Blues in Thirds").

Long is the list, Jelly Roll Morton and Wilhelm Backhaus, Monique Haas and Arthur Rubinstein, Bud Powell and Dinu Lipatti. The monstrous hands of Alexander Brailowsky, the tiny ones of Clara Haskil, that way of listening to herself that Margarita Fernández had, the splendid implosion of Friedrich Gulda into the Buenos Aires habits of the forties, Walter Gieseking, Georges Arvanitas, the unknown pianist in a bar in Kampala, Don Sebas-

tián Piana and his milongas, Maurizio Pollini and
Marian McPartland, amidst unpardonable forget-
fulness and reasons to cut off a roster that would
end in weariness, Schnabel, Ingrid Haebler, Solo-
mon nights, Ronnie Scott's bar in London where
someone who was going back to the piano was on
the point of pouring a glass of beer onto Lucas's
woman's hair and that someone was Thelonious,
Thelonious Sphere, Thelonious Sphere Monk.

At the hour of his death, if there is time and
lucidity, Lucas will ask to hear two things: Mozart's
last quintet and a certain piano solo on the theme of
"I Ain't Got Nobody." If he feels that there won't
be enough time, he'll only ask for the piano record.
Long is the list, but he's already chosen. Out of the
depths of time, Earl Hines will accompany him.

Lucas, His Long Marches

Everybody knows that the earth is separated from other heavenly bodies by a variable number of light years. What few know (in reality, only I) is that Margarita is separated from me by a considerable number of snail years.

At first I thought it was a matter of tortoise years, but I've had to abandon that unit of measurement as too flattering. Little as a tortoise may travel, I would have ended up reaching Margarita, but, on the other hand, Osvaldo, my favorite snail, doesn't leave me the slightest hope. Who knows when he started the march that was imperceptibly taking him farther away from my left shoe, even though I had oriented him with extreme precision in the direction that would lead him to Margarita. Full of fresh lettuce, care, and lovingly attended, his first advance was promising, and I said to myself hopefully that before the patio pine passed beyond the height of the roof, Osvaldo's silver-plated horns would enter Margarita's field of vision to bring her my friendly message; in the meantime, from here I could be happy imagining her joy on seeing him arrive, the waving of her braids and arms.

All light years may be equal, but not so snail years, and Osvaldo has ceased to merit my trust. It isn't that he's stopped, since it's possible for me to verify by his silvery trail that he's continuing his march and that he's maintaining the right direction, although this presupposes his going up and down countless walls or passing completely through a noodle factory. But it's been more difficult for me to check that meritorious exactness, and twice I've been stopped by furious watchmen to whom I've had to tell the worst lies since the truth would have brought me a rain of whacks. The sad part is that Margarita, sitting in a pink velvet easy chair, is waiting for me on the other side of the city. If instead of Osvaldo I had made use of light years, we probably would already have had grandchildren; but when one loves long and softly, when one wants to come to the end of a drawn-out wait, it's logical that snail years should be chosen. It's so hard, after all, to decide on what the advantages and the disadvantages of these options are.

A NOTE ON THE TYPE

The text of this book was set in Electra, a typeface
designed by William Addison Dwiggins for the
Mergenthaler Linotype Company and first made
available in 1935. Electra cannot be classified
as either "modern" or "old style." It is not based on
any historical model and hence does not echo any
particular period or style of type design. It
avoids the extreme contrast between thick and thin
elements that marks most modern faces and is
without eccentricities that catch the eye and
interfere with reading. In general, Electra is a simple,
readable typeface that attempts to give a feeling of
fluidity, power, and speed.

Composed by Maryland Linotype Composition
Company, Inc., Baltimore, Maryland.
Printed and bound by The Haddon Craftsmen, Inc.,
Scranton, Pennsylvania.

Designed by Judith Henry.